THE MISSING HOURS

ALSO BY JULIA DAHL

Conviction

Run You Down

Invisible City

THE MISSING HOURS

Julia Dahl

MINOTAUR
BOOKS
NEW YORK

This is a work of fiction. All of the characters, organizations, and events portrayed in this novel are either products of the author's imagination or are used fictitiously.

First published in the United States by Minotaur Books, an imprint of St. Martin's Publishing Group

www.minotaurbooks.com

Designed by Omar Chapa

Library of Congress Cataloging-in-Publication Data

Names: Dahl, Julia, 1977– author.
Title: The missing hours / Julia Dahl.
Description: First Edition. | New York : Minotaur Books, 2021.
Identifiers: LCCN 2021015667 | ISBN 9781250083722 (hardcover) | ISBN 9781250083739 (ebook)
Subjects: GSAFD: Mystery fiction.
Classification: LCC PS3604.A339 M57 2021 | DDC 813/.6—dc23
LC record available at https://lccn.loc.gov/2021015667

First Edition: 2021

10 9 8 7 6 5 4 3 2 1

For my sister

PART 1

CLAUDIA

The details of whatever happened were gone from her mind, but present all over her body. Claudia dropped her hand below the stiff dorm bed and felt for a water bottle. It was nearly empty, but she sucked the liquid down and it was enough to get her sitting. Upright, there was pain. Her skirt was bunched around her waist, and her underwear was gone. She stood and as she took off the skirt she noticed it was damp. Claudia brought it to her face, then recoiled: unmistakably urine. But the bed wasn't wet. In the corner of the room she found a pair of shorts. She pulled them on and dragged herself across the common area to the bathroom.

When she sat on the toilet Claudia cried out. The sting was shocking and prolonged; the soreness deep as a canyon. She was going get a UTI. *Do I have a pill for that?* That was the first question she asked herself. And the answer was no.

She'd used the last one when she hooked up with Ben Herman over Christmas and never managed to call in a refill. So, it was going to be a call to her family's doctor, who might mention the request to her mother. Or a visit to NYU's health center. The health center made her think of herpes. *Did he use a condom?* That was the first question she couldn't answer. Because, who was he?

There was no paper on the roll and when she looked down she saw blood. Claudia feebly wiggled her hips and pulled up the shorts.

When she filled up the water bottle at the sink Claudia had to confront the mirror. Her lip was split and had bled onto her chin. Her right eyelid was purple, swollen half shut. She stood in the windowless bathroom for a long time, waiting for the shock to fade. Waiting to find something familiar in the face there. But the familiar was gone.

She ran the water until it was warm, cupped her hands beneath the tap, and brought them to her face. Twice, three times. She rubbed lightly and the caked red on her chin loosened, ran pink into the sink. *Where can I hide until this goes away?* As much as it sucked, the dorm—mostly empty for spring break—was probably best.

She pushed aside the moldy shower curtain and turned the tap to hot.

EDIE

Claudia was supposed to be in the room for the birth. The doula had suggested Edie Castro choose one person to hold each leg, and she'd picked her new husband, Nathan, and her little sister. But when Edie called from the backseat of the taxi traveling up First Avenue, Claudia's phone just rang and rang.

"It's me," Edie said to the voice mail. "My water broke. I'm on my way."

She hung up and texted the same message.

A contraction came and she stretched back, trying to straighten her legs, as if she could make the cramp spread out; curl her toes instead of her writhing middle. Nathan reached for her hand and hit the button on the app to record the duration of her pain. It was just after midnight. Outside the windows the lights of the city smeared by.

They pulled up to Emergency and Nathan jogged in to get a wheelchair.

Edie texted her parents and Claudia again from the intake area. Once they got in a room, Nathan set up a laptop and a speaker, but there were only four songs on the birth playlist they'd started back in January. Neither of them were ready for this.

But Claudia didn't rattle. When Claudia got here, it would be all right.

An hour passed and Edie lost count of the strangers coming in and going out of the room, looking at the monitor she was attached to, helping her squat over a bin to pee. Finally, just after dawn, the doctor asked if she felt like she should start pushing. At 7:07 a.m., a 5-pound 9-ounce little girl came shooting out into the world, squint-eyed and crying. Edie was crying, too, her arm thrown over her eyes. They sewed her up and put the baby on her chest. Edie looked down and saw the hair on the girl's head. What was she supposed to feel? What was she supposed to do? Where was Claudia?

The nurses took the baby to be inspected, and Edie and Nathan were alone in the room for the first time since they'd arrived. She was supposed to have given birth in their little rental house in Poughkeepsie with the midwife she'd chosen. She was supposed to be surrounded by candles. She was supposed to be able to lay her head back on her own pillows and gaze at the photographs she'd taken of the places and people who made her feel happy and strong. But that plan dissolved when her mother had announced that if Edie didn't have the baby in the city, at "the best" hospital, she'd lose access to her trust fund. So now she was shivering in a room where the lights never seemed to go down and the machines never stopped buzzing. She closed her eyes and asked Nathan for a blanket.

"I can't believe how great you did," he said.

Edie kept her eyes shut. She tried to give him a smile but it probably looked like a wince.

"Have you checked my phone?" she asked.

"Claudia hasn't called. But I looked at her Instagram."

Edie opened her eyes. "What?"

"She went out last night."

"Let me see."

He handed her his phone. Claudia's last post was a selfie (*#staycation #springbreak #nyc*) uploaded at 11:04 p.m. from a bar on Bleecker. An hour before Edie texted from the cab. Her sister looked drunk in the photo; her eyelids low, her mouth captured in a scream-smile. *Yes! Look at me! I'm having so much fun!* They'd talked about this exact thing two days ago. Two days! *I could go at any time*, Edie said. *Make sure you have your phone.* It was hard to wrap her mind around it: Claudia had missed the birth. All the arrangements, the fucking *class* they took together—and her sister just got wasted.

The nurses wheeled the baby back in a plastic bassinet, swaddled tight and sleeping.

"Has someone started you expressing yet?" asked the nurse. Edie shook her head. The nurse told her to squeeze her breast. "Like you're trying to get frosting out of a tube." She held a tiny plastic cup beneath Edie's nipple, but nothing came out. "Keep trying," said the nurse. "It can take some women a while. Kept switching breasts."

A few minutes later, Edie's father, Gabriel Castro, peeked in the door.

"Can I come in?"

Edie pulled her gown back up over her shoulder. Her dad's hair was rumpled; he was wearing a Pavement T-shirt, jeans, and an old pair of Vans. Millions of dollars and half a dozen Grammys after leaving dusty Central California, her dad still dressed like a boy who'd just gotten off a cross-country bus. Six months ago, Edie's mom, Michelle Whitehouse, had announced that after more than half a life together, she was leaving him. So that boy was now almost fifty, graying, and alone. As far as Edie could tell, her dad hadn't left the family's town house in a month. But when Nathan set the swaddled child in her father's arms, he giggled. He couldn't contain the happiness the little person she'd made gave him. That was something, thought Edie. Had she made the right decision keeping the baby? This was a check in the "yes" box.

"Does she have a name?" Gabe asked.

"I think Edie wanted to wait till you guys were all together to tell everybody," said Nathan. He looked at Edie, who shrugged. What was the point of a big reveal? Claudia was probably passed out in some asshole's bed, and her mom, well, she could go fuck herself.

"Lydia," said Edie. "Lydia Castro McHugh."

Gabe looked down at the baby and put a finger on top

of her ear, just peeking up from the swaddle. "Hello, little Lydia. Welcome to New York City." He looked up at Edie, eyes glassy. "It's a beautiful name. She's beautiful. Nathan, we're surrounded by beautiful women."

Nathan smiled. He was sitting beside Edie and he leaned forward, kissed her on the cheek. For the next hour, Gabe held sleeping Lydia. He paced the room, he sat on the pink-and-blue loveseat, he whispered in her ear as he looked out the window at the city below. It was Saturday, and traffic on the FDR was light. The sun shone off the East River and the Roosevelt Island tram carried people across in a glass capsule. When Lydia woke and started to cry, he handed her to Edie and asked, "Where's your sister?"

TREVOR

Claudia Castro walked right into him as she came out of the elevator. Trevor was in sleep shorts and shower sandals. He'd run out of toothpaste and was headed to get some at the Rite-Aid on University.

"Whoa!" he said. She stumbled back, her sunglasses falling to the floor. Trevor took in her broken face. "Oh my gosh, are you okay?"

He bent down to pick up the glasses.

"I'm so sorry," he continued when she didn't answer. "We've got a first aid kit in our room."

"I'm okay," she said, taking the glasses without looking up. "Thanks."

She walked past him. Limped, actually. Favoring one leg, bent slightly at the waist like she had a cramp. Trevor watched her go—he couldn't help it. Perfect little half-moons peeked beneath the edge of her shorts. Her butt was small, but it moved just enough that he felt it. After the drugstore, he got in the shower and rubbed one out before church.

On his way back to the dorm, Trevor stopped at a café on MacDougal and ordered coffee and a blueberry muffin—everybody likes those, right? Unless she was gluten free. Or vegan. Trevor didn't know many vegans in Canton, but a lot of the girls he met since arriving in New York had some dietary restriction or another. Either way, it was a gesture. Her roommate, Whitney, who he'd been hooking up with for a couple months, was big on gestures. Hopefully Claudia was, too.

"It's Trevor," he said after knocking at her door. He smiled into the peephole. "I live down the hall. We bumped into each other earlier."

Claudia opened the door just a few inches. She was still wearing the sunglasses, but they didn't cover all the wounds on her face.

"There's cream and sugar in the bag," said Trevor, raising the coffee.

She looked puzzled, like he'd changed the subject.

"I'm Trevor," he heard himself say again.

Claudia accepted the coffee and the brown paper bag with the muffin inside.

"Thanks," she said, and shut the door.

At the little desk in his bedroom, Trevor tried to focus on his paper for Comparative Religion. He was writing about the concept of nirvana in Buddhism. It had to be six pages and use at least four primary sources, but he gave up after two hours and barely a page. He was supposed to be imagining a life free of spiritual poison, but all he could see was Claudia Castro's face.

She knocked on his door that evening.

"Hey," she said. "I'm Claudia."

Trevor smiled, too big, probably. But whatever. He was happy to see her.

"Are you going back out?" she asked.

"I could."

"I'm sorry to ask but is there any way I could give you some money to go to the drugstore? I can't find my phone and I don't really want to run into anybody."

"Sure."

"Thanks." She handed him a hundred-dollar bill and a list handwritten on the back of a subscription card for *Marie Claire* magazine. "No rush or anything. I just . . ."

"You don't have to explain," said Trevor. "Do you want some dinner, too? I was gonna get ramen."

"Yeah?"

He nodded. It wasn't exactly a lie. He had been planning on ramen for dinner, but the plan involved microwaving a dollar-packet from their common room cabinet microwaved with bathroom sink water, not the $20 bowls they sold at the Japanese place down the block.

"Sure," she said. "I'd take some rice and veggies. Thanks."

An hour later, Trevor knocked on her door.

"Delivery."

"I really appreciate it," said Claudia. She was still wearing the sunglasses.

He paused after handing her the food. He wanted to ask what happened. Somehow, he sensed he could help.

"Do you want to come in?" she asked.

They ate at the coffee table. Claudia was quiet and he looked around the room for something to talk about. Trevor had been here to hook up with Whitney, but they spent most of the time in her bed. For Whitney, Claudia was the Holy Grail of roommates: rarely there. *She's rich,* Whitney told him as an explanation. On a chair near the window Trevor saw an oversized leather portfolio case and he remembered that Whitney mentioned Claudia took art classes. But he didn't know anything about art and he didn't want to say something stupid, so the silence continued until Claudia asked why he was still on campus over spring break.

"I've got a lot of work to catch up on." Again, not a lie, but not the whole truth. The whole truth was that he hadn't raised enough money to go to Costa Rica and build houses with his church group. His parents would have liked to see him, but going home was exhausting and flights expensive. "What about you?"

"Obviously, I should have gotten out of town."

She didn't elaborate. He noticed her water glass was empty so he got up and refilled it, then gathered their takeout detritus and bagged it.

"I should go to bed," she said.

"Cool. Thanks for dinner." *Stupid*, he thought. *I brought it to her.*

CLAUDIA

After the boy from down the hall left, Claudia called the security desk downstairs and was told, for the third time, that no one had turned in her phone. It had been twenty-four hours and she still had no idea how she'd gotten back to bed, or who she'd been with past eleven o'clock the night before.

She'd blacked out only one other time, on Martha's Vineyard last summer. After a graduation dinner at a restaurant near their seaside estate, Claudia's parents had allowed her to stay and drink with her twenty-two-year-old sister, Edie. The bartender made key lime martinis and after two they stumbled down to the yacht club at the Edgartown harbor. Alcohol, the great equalizer: The prep school kids from Boston and New York were sharing a bottle of vodka with the barbacks and servers who worked on the island. The last thing she remembered was accepting someone's coat around her shoulders. The next morning, after she woke up in a deck chair, her sister informed her that at some point she'd announced to everyone she wasn't going to let anybody fuck her until college.

"You said it was going to be the 'Summer of Blow Jobs!'" howled Edie.

"No, I didn't," said Claudia, although it sounded like something she might say, especially if she was drunk.

"Nathan is a witness," said Edie.

"It's true," said Nathan, Edie's scruffy boyfriend from Vassar. He'd spent the summer with them and knocked Edie up that August, right under their parents' noses.

They were all sitting in the breakfast room, a wall of French doors flung open onto the stone patio. The pool, the grass, the sand, the ocean, the blue sky: Claudia could stand up and run straight into the horizon from the table.

"You were pretty messed up," said her sister. "I thought you went off to puke, but you never came back."

"You didn't try to find me?"

"I figured you'd go home, and I was right."

"I don't even remember getting here."

"You probably blacked out," said Nathan.

Before that night, Claudia had assumed people who said they didn't remember what happened when they were drunk were lying. Or at least they weren't being literal. The idea that she'd said and done things she had no memory of was disturbing—and, in the case of her alleged Edgartown exclamation, mildly humiliating—but sitting alone in her dorm room now, staring into the black hole in her mind, she realized she hadn't even considered how lucky she'd been that night on the island. She could have fallen off the dock, hit her head on one of the night-silent boats, and been washed away by the black water. She could have tripped stumbling home and gotten hit by a sleepy driver. She could have been raped.

Claudia took three Benadryls and slept for twelve hours on the shitty dorm mattress, dreaming of banging on doors and falling down stairs. In the morning the fear became more acute: the infection was coming. She needed the pills and she needed to find her phone.

Trevor knocked about an hour later, while she was working up the courage to go outside.

"I'm on my way to the library," he said. "I can pick something up if you want."

He was very good-looking: symmetrical features, clear skin, dark brown eyes, a hint of muscle beneath his T-shirt. As he waited for her answer, Trevor fiddled with the chain on his neck, revealing a simple gold cross. A week ago, Claudia would have considered hooking up with him, even though she was pretty sure her roommate already was. A week ago, she would have taken in his scent and imagined what he tasted like. She might have smiled and flirted and wondered if he could make her stop thinking about Ben for a little while. But not now. Now there were whole pieces of her that seemed to have been swept away. Why couldn't she remember? Claudia looked at Trevor and thought: *I need to get outside.*

"I'm gonna head out, too," she said. She looked around. Wallet, sunglasses, hat. Was that all she needed? "Maybe the sun will feel good."

"I bet it will," he said.

But it didn't. The dehydration that had sucked at her brain the day before was quenched, as was the woozy slosh of alcohol in her stomach. But that delicate feeling of a hangover remained. The very air felt aggressive and the missing hours thrashed behind her eyes. The hole in her mind seemed to have its own gravity.

"Are you going anywhere specific?" Trevor asked as they walked toward Broadway.

"The health center," she said.

"I went once for a flu shot. I bet it won't be crowded now, since it's spring break."

Claudia looked at him. He was imagining her concerns and trying to allay them. He barely knew her and yet he cared enough to consider not just what she might want to eat, but what she might be worried about. Claudia didn't know many people like that. They walked side by side, not speaking. On the next block, they passed the green-and-pink neon sign for a bubble tea shop, and it ignited a pinprick of light in the darkness of her memory. She saw her hands on the sidewalk, felt an arm around her waist, and the cool night air under her too-short skirt.

"I fell," she said.

"What?"

Whose arm was it? "Never mind."

She kept walking. He probably thought she was insane.

"Do you want me to go with you?" Trevor asked. "I've just got reading. I can do it there."

Why did she say yes? Because she trusted him? Because she wanted an audience? Her sister was off social media since getting pregnant and routinely accused Claudia of needing an audience for every moment of her life. *I don't need anything*, Claudia protested. *It's just fun*.

From outside the glass entrance doors she scanned the waiting room and didn't see anyone she recognized. She told the receptionist she needed to see a nurse to get some medication and was handed a clipboard.

"Don't forget to fill out both sides."

Claudia kept her sunglasses on as she sat beside Trevor in a deep plastic chair. She began filling out the boxes: name, birth date, student ID number, medications. Are you pregnant? Have you ever been pregnant? Do you use alcohol? If so, how much? Do you use other intoxicating substances? She finished the paperwork, signed away her privacy, returned the clipboard to the receptionist, and sat back down. The magazines on the side table next to her were awful. Princess Meghan and Kylie Jenner and Cardi B. *Blah Blah Blah.* She pushed them aside and picked up yesterday's copy of the *New York Post.* SUBWAY SLASHER STRIKES AGAIN screamed the headline, the ink red and the font appropriating a cheesy horror movie poster.

"Did you see this?" she asked Trevor.

He leaned over. "Yeah, I got an alert on my phone this morning."

"An alert?"

"From the university. I guess it happened at the Astor Place station. My parents are kind of freaking out. I keep telling them I basically never go anywhere except class."

Claudia put the paper down. *It could have been worse,* she thought. At least she didn't get stabbed.

"Ms. Castro?"

A nurse with short blond hair and skinny arms held open a door for her.

"I'll be here when you get back," said Trevor.

In exam room 2, the nurse sat on a wheeled stool and pulled a wall-mounted computer monitor toward her.

"What can I help you with today?" she asked, typing.

"I need some Cipro," said Claudia. The paper on the exam table crunched beneath her. "I have a UTI."

"You've taken it before?"

"Yes."

"Would you mind taking off your sunglasses?"

Claudia hesitated. But what was she going to do, refuse?

"That looks recent," said the nurse, frowning. She lifted a black flashlight off the wall. "Do you mind if I take a look?"

Claudia didn't protest. The nurse donned rubber gloves, placed her fingers on Claudia's face, and shone a thin beam of light into her eye.

"How's your vision?"

"Fine."

The nurse put the light back on the wall. Claudia noticed a tattoo on the inside of her left arm: a thin arrow pointing toward her wrist. She'd seen those before. Supposedly they represented forward movement; struggles overcome. Claudia wondered what the tattoo meant to the nurse. What had she gone through before having it inked into her skin? Was it over now?

"When did this happen?" asked the nurse, peering at Claudia's face.

"The night before last."

"Same incident as the lip?"

Claudia nodded. She needed to make something up.

"I was drunk. I tripped and fell onto a . . ." A what? "A coffee table."

The nurse didn't laugh, which Claudia appreciated.

"Must have been a hard fall," she said. "Have you ever injured yourself while intoxicated before?"

"No," said Claudia.

"Was anyone with you?"

"Um, yeah."

"Have you spoken with them? If we know exactly what happened it'll help guide your care."

"I haven't," said Claudia. "I lost my phone."

The nurse nodded. She was waiting for details, if Claudia wanted to provide them. Would she, if she knew?

"You can get an ice pack at CVS. Wrap it in a towel and hold it over the eye and the lip as often as you can handle. Try not to touch either too much otherwise. You really don't want the eye to get infected."

"How long until it goes away?"

"A few days for the lip. Probably a week, maybe a little more, on the eye."

Edie's due date was in a week.

"Tell me about your other symptoms," said the nurse.

"Symptoms?"

"You said you thought you had a UTI."

"Right." The reason she was here. "I pretty much always get them after sex."

"When did you last have intercourse?"

"The night before last."

The words hung in the air. Claudia diverted her eyes. Did she look as stupid as she felt?

"Would you mind telling me your symptoms?" asked the nurse. "I don't want to alarm you, but occasionally symptoms of sexually transmitted infections mirror those of UTIs."

"Oh. Um. It stings when I pee. And I feel like I have to go a lot." The last part wasn't true, but it would be if she didn't get the pill.

"Did your partner use a condom?"

Claudia hesitated. "I'm not sure."

"Would you like to go ahead and do STI testing then? Just in case?"

"Okay." Her eyes stung. She was not going to cry. But she understood. STI meant STD. Sluts got STDs. She'd seen the scare pictures in sex ed. The sores and the foul smells and the snickers forever behind her back. She was not that girl. She was not that girl.

"It's a blood test and a urine sample. Shouldn't take long at all. What about birth control? Would you like Plan B today?"

"Okay." She was on the Pill, but had she remembered to take it that night? Or the night before? Or last night?

"Do you have any reason to think your partner might be HIV positive?" asked the nurse.

"What?" Sweat popped open the pores on her neck, beneath her arms. Her breath quickened.

"If you think you might be at risk we can get you on PrEP. It's one pill a day for twenty-eight days. It's not one hundred percent, but if you start within seventy-two hours of exposure and take it as directed we think it's very effective."

"Okay." Claudia tried to swallow but her tongue stuck to the roof of her mouth. The nurse was talking about AIDS. She might have AIDS.

"Is this the first time you've had unprotected sex?" asked the nurse.

"Yeah. I guess it is. Was."

"Was it a new partner?"

"Um . . ." The nurse waited, but Claudia couldn't think of what else to say. She felt like she was shrinking.

"Was alcohol involved?"

Claudia nodded. "I've only ever blacked out once before."

"Do you think that's what happened? You blacked out from drinking?"

"I don't really remember."

"Would you say you think the sex was consensual, then?"

"Consensual?"

"If you were incapacitated, do you think you were the victim of an assault?"

Claudia didn't answer. She remembered dinner with Lolly and Adrienne Kennedy, the twins she'd gone to prep school with. But after that there was nothing.

"Claudia?"

"I don't know." It took everything she had not to scream it.

"Okay. If you're willing, I recommend the STI tests, and the PrEP, just in case. Have you ever used it before?"

Claudia shook her head.

"The side effects are minimal, but you do have to take it every day for the whole twenty-eight days for it to be effective."

"Okay." She sounded like a moron: *okay okay okay.* She should have questions; she did have questions, but she seemed to have lost the ability to ask them. Nearly lost the ability to speak.

"If you think you might have been assaulted, there are other, more specialized tests that can help us preserve any evidence that may still be available. We can't do that here, but the Wellness Project has counselors that can meet you at the hospital and make sure you're supported. I'll be honest, the test is invasive. But if you think you might want to report what happened, it's helpful. And I don't want to pressure you, but the sooner you get it done the better."

The nurse swiveled on her stool and took a brochure from a plastic bin on the wall.

"Have you showered since the night before last?"

Claudia nodded. Finally, she understood. How many *SVU* episodes had she seen? What was the mantra for every special victim? Don't wash the evidence away. But she had.

"What we'd be able to collect might be limited, but if you want to make a report I still recommend it. There might be something there. Either way, if you want to talk, call the hotline. I've trained some of the girls myself and it can be really helpful to talk after something . . . confusing, has happened. You'd be surprised—or maybe you wouldn't be—how many people end up in situations like this. Especially freshman year."

Claudia took the brochure. It was NYU purple and white. A line drawing of a woman's profile. A phone number and website. She'd been given the same brochure probably a dozen times in the first few months of school. She imagined them piled inside trash cans across the Village.

"Okay, so we'll do the blood and urine." The nurse paused. "We've got lots of resources here. And if you want to talk—even if you're just feeling confused, the Wellness Project is really great."

Claudia nodded. "Thanks."

The nurse came back with PrEP, Cipro, a Plan B pack, and a pee cup.

"We keep the popular items stocked," said the nurse, possibly attempting humor.

She pointed to the bathroom and instructed Claudia to use the Sharpie to label the cup, then leave it on the tray when she was done, and return to the room to have her blood drawn. Claudia took the medication and the cup and nodded, then walked out of the health center.

TREVOR

"Claudia!"

Trevor called from the sidewalk and Claudia stopped abruptly in front of a Chase bank where a man was muttering at the ATM, jamming his card in and out. He turned around and shouted *"Back up!"* Claudia jumped, scurried forward, stopped again.

"Are you okay?" he asked.

For a second, she seemed not to recognize him.

"Is everything okay?" Stop saying okay, he thought. She is clearly not okay. "I think you left your sunglasses in there."

Her hand went to her face. "Fuck. *Fuck.*" Her voice shook, the pitch higher than he remembered. Trevor wondered what they'd told her in the health center. Some of the swelling seemed to have gone down but her eyeball was swimming with cherry-Slurpee-red blood. The skin around it looked painted purple.

"Here," said Trevor, lifting his sunglasses from where they hung at the neck of his T-shirt.

She put them on. "Thank you."

They walked in silence toward the dorm. Would she tell him if she wanted to be alone? When they were back in the lobby, the guard stopped Claudia.

"Somebody found a phone in the stairwell," he said. "What kind of cover does yours have?"

"Silver."

The guard reached beneath the desk and brought out the latest iPhone model. "Is this it?"

"Yes," said Claudia. "Thanks."

"It just rang," said the guard. "You've got a lot of missed calls."

Claudia unlocked the phone and scrolled. Trevor couldn't see the reaction in her eyes, but her mouth dropped open and she drew in air.

"My sister had her baby," she said. "My sister had her baby and I wasn't there."

"Shit," said the guard. "That sucks."

"Shut up, man," said Trevor. He put a hand on her shoulder and she let him lead her to the elevator.

"What am I going to tell her?" Claudia asked as the doors closed.

"Just explain what happened."

"I don't know what happened. Not really. The nurse asked and I had to make something up."

They got off the elevator and he followed her to her room.

"You said you fell," said Trevor.

"I fell, yeah. But that's not what happened."

"You lost your phone. She'll understand. I mean, once she sees you. She's your sister."

Even as he said it, he realized he was overstepping. What did he know about her family? Trevor trusted his brother, Mike, even if most people didn't. If Trevor had gotten into something that ended in his face looking like Claudia's, he'd have gone to Mike. But not everybody had that with family.

Claudia unlocked the door to her suite and walked straight to the sink. She filled a glass of water then sat on the sofa and laid several sets of pills in front of her on the coffee table. She pushed the pills out of the packets, put them all in her mouth, and swallowed.

"I'm gonna lie down," she said.

"I'll be around. Let me know if you need anything."

Back in his room, Trevor Googled Claudia Castro. She had nearly twenty thousand followers on Instagram, and the last time she'd posted was the night before they'd met. The night whatever happened to her happened to her. The photo was a selfie taken from that elevated angle girls use that makes them look vulnerable when they're actually entirely in control. The caption read: *#springbreak #staycation #nyc*. There were other selfies in the feed, too, and some weird art. Wikipedia said her dad was a music producer who had worked with Beck and Rihanna and the Strokes and won a bunch of Grammys. Her mom had been a model, the daughter of a senator who died in a plane crash. He followed some links to old gossip items about Claudia's parents, who apparently: never married but had been together for more than two decades. There were pictures of them with Johnny Depp and Kate Moss, Jennifer Lopez and Puffy, and an article about someone in a London hotel calling the police because of their "loud sex." There were images of Claudia and her sister, Edie or Eden, depending on the captions, posing beneath white tents, in front of banners, on boats; with friends, boyfriends, celebrities. Edie appeared taller than Claudia in most, but they could have been twins with their long brown hair and golden-flecked eyes. Right after the New Year, Claudia was named one of *Manhattan* magazine's Most Beautiful New Yorkers under Twenty-five. The magazine called her an "art patron, student" and linked to a six-year-old article from the *New York Post*:

TEEN HEIRESS TURNS $1K TO $1M

By Ronnie Benson

"She just has an eye."

That's what Grammy-winning producer Gabriel Castro says of his now 13-year-old daughter, Claudia, who spotted talent in mixed-media artist Roderick Masters before most art world insiders had even heard of him.

And now she's turned that "eye" into an eye-popping windfall.

Claudia was just 12 when she and her father visited Masters' Ridgewood studio last spring.

"We were studying contemporary art in school and there was an assignment to visit an 'unknown' artist's studio," explains the precocious prep-school student, whose teacher at Manchester Academy calls Claudia a "budding artist herself."

Claudia says she'd seen some of Masters' work at a Brooklyn art fair the Christmas before, and after the studio visit asked her parents if they could buy an intricate bronze piece depicting two men playing chess in a park, surrounded by onlookers.

"We told her if she wanted it, she'd have to use the money she'd saved from gifts," said Castro's mother, Michelle Whitehouse.

She did, and a few months later a curator for the New Museum noticed the piece while at the family's Gramercy town house for a dinner party.

"It stopped me cold," said Jelissa Homan. "I made Claudia tell me everything about the artist."

Within days, Homan arranged for Masters to be included in an exhibition at the New Museum, and acquired two sculptures for the museum's permanent collection and one for herself.

"Claudia has a genuine gift for spotting artistic talent," said Homan. "If I could hire her, I would."

Asked why she decided now was the time to sell Chess, Claudia told the Post that when the offer came in—from a private collector the family declined to name—she knew it would be stupid to turn it down.

"It's really good for the artist to have a sale like that," she said.

As for what she plans to do with her more than one million dollars in profit, Claudia didn't hesitate to answer: "Buy more art."

The most recent links were nastier. A couple weeks ago, Claudia apparently appeared on an episode of a reality show that had filmed last summer. Trevor clicked on a clip of *Rich Kids: The Hamptons* and saw her jumping into a swimming pool at a party. A boy jumped in after her and they batted at each other, her face gleeful, animated with an energy she didn't seem to possess now. The camera cut to another girl narrating the scene, telling the audience that the boy in the pool was her boyfriend and that Claudia "threw herself at him." The show cut back to the party, but a different scene. The camera appeared hidden in some bushes, and the image, while not as sharp, was clear: Claudia was making out with the boy from the pool. She was wet and loose, obviously enjoying the encounter. Trevor felt himself get hard. He clicked out of the video.

The next morning, Claudia knocked on his door and offered a cup of coffee from the machine downstairs. Then she asked if she could hang out and study.

"Sure," he said. If his smile was too big she didn't notice—or at least she didn't seem to. She sat down on the sofa, pulled her legs beneath her, and unfolded the case on an iPad.

"Did you text your sister?" he asked.

"Yeah," she said.

He waited but she offered nothing else. He tried again. "What are you working on?

"Art history. They test you with slides. Like, when was this made, and by who, and what does it represent."

"You're into art?"

She sighed. "I am. But I'm shitty at it."

"I doubt that."

"No, it's true. I mean, I'm competent. But I've never really had anything to say. Art's about ideas."

"It is?"

"Well, not just ideas. The combination of idea and execution. And then, something else. Something you can't really name. Like a spirit, sort of. Or like umami."

"Ooh-what?"

Claudia smiled. It was the first time she'd smiled since they met. Was it worth it, that he made her smile with his ignorance? "Umami. In food. It's that extra thing that takes it from good to *delicious.*"

"Okay."

"One of my drawings is in the library on Martha's Vineyard, but nobody would put it in a real gallery. And nobody would, like, pay for it."

"The library's pretty cool. And you're young. I mean, isn't part of making art having life experience?"

"Yeah," she said. "So, you know a little, too."

"I probably heard that in a movie."

Claudia laughed and Trevor's chest warmed. They went back to studying and a few hours later, Trevor ran out to pick up dinner. They watched an episode of *The Marvelous Mrs. Maisel* while they ate and Claudia pointed out her former babysitter in one of the scenes. Around nine, Claudia said she was tired, and went back to her room. That was how they spent the rest of the week. Eating and studying and watching TV. It was hard to square the girl he'd found online with the girl he got to know over those quiet days. The girl still wearing his borrowed sunglasses and picking the cilantro out of the burrito bowls he brought up from Chipotle. He was attracted to her in a way he couldn't articulate, and in a way that transcended the particulars of her objective beauty. She sat differently than girls he knew, reached for a fork differently, gathered her hair into a ponytail differently. He couldn't keep his eyes off her. She was so much more beautiful than the person in the makeup and dresses on the Internet. He wondered how many other people knew this Claudia Castro. He let himself feel special that she showed him this part of her; he let himself think that it meant something.

They never talked about whatever happened the night before they bumped into each other, and as the physical evidence faded, so did the topic as an obvious point of conversation. Trevor wondered if, once she looked normal again, she would drop him. He had no claim on her. They'd never so much as held hands. Never even hugged. There was a certain energy when they were together, but Trevor knew what he felt was his own, and that while to him it might feel big enough to fill a room, that didn't mean it existed inside her at all. He'd never been in this position before. He didn't like it, but he wasn't going to ruin it. He'd seen peers push a "friend" to something more and have it blow up in their faces. Trevor would wait. And hope.

EDIE

Lydia was thirty-six hours old when Claudia finally called. Edie hadn't slept since giving birth and when the phone rang, its trill muffled beneath a pile of jackets and tote bags, she didn't hear it—or if she did, she mistook the noise for one of the constantly beeping machines in her hospital room. Various nurses had spent much of the day instructing her on how to squeeze her breast to "express" her milk—but so far, Edie's body emitted nothing more than a trickle of a snot-like substance that the nurse called *colostrum*.

"Keep trying," said Oris, a tall woman with a thick Caribbean accent and Hello Kitty faces on her scrubs. She scraped the colostrum from the tip of Edie's nipple into a tiny plastic cup, then drew it into a blunt-tipped syringe. "All the good stuff's in there."

Edie's feet itched inside the hospital-issue socks. She was

wearing a hero-sized maxi pad and gauze underwear. Her eyes were dry and her brain felt both swollen and shriveled. All night long, while Nathan slept on the two-tone love seat beside her, she stared at the TV, watching couples hunt for houses by the beach, vaguely following their happy journeys through blurry closed captions. She kept her phone in her hand the whole time, waiting for Claudia to call. One minute she was livid, offended, disgusted that her sister would abandon her at the most intense moment of her life. The next minute, she was frantic, her body drowning in adrenaline as she searched her mind for where her sister could be. Claudia liked to walk by the water; could she have gotten drunk and slipped off a pier at South Street Seaport? Could she have been kidnapped by an Uber driver?

Oris lifted Lydia from the bassinet and handed the baby and the syringe to Edie. As she slid the tip between Lydia's lips, Nathan walked in carrying a bag from the Greek diner a block away. While pregnant, Edie wasn't allowed to eat an astonishing number of the foods she loved, and in the bag was one she'd missed the most: a runny egg and cheese sandwich. Nathan kissed her on the head and watched as Lydia drank the gooey serum. Oris suggested she try, again, to get the baby to latch.

"Tickle under baby's chin," said the nurse. "Tilt her. Yes. Now use your finger to open baby's mouth."

Edie felt like she didn't have enough hands to do what she was being told. Hold baby. Tilt baby. Tickle baby. Open baby's mouth. Squeeze the breast. Keep baby upright. Support baby's head. She fumbled, looking down at her enormous areola, trying to shove it all far enough back into Lydia's mouth that it wouldn't just drop right out. It dropped right out.

"Fuck," she hissed, tears burning her eyes.

"Try to relax," said Oris. "Try again."

Lydia started to squirm. She shook her head, screwed up her face, and let out a mewl. A mewl Edie was beginning to recognize as the harbinger of a wail.

"Baby's hungry," said Oris. "Time to eat."

Edie had never felt more helpless. What did this woman expect her to do?

"Baby needs to eat. Here we go. Use the nipple to tickle her bottom lip."

The wailing began. Nathan stood beside her, watching. Oris, watching.

"Come on now," said Oris.

"You can do it," said Nathan.

"Obviously I can't!"

"Hold your breast," said Oris. Edie could barely see through the tears. She could taste the runoff from her nose. "Hold your breast and I'll hold baby. There. Yes. There. Now hold her head. Hold her head! Yes! Keep holding!"

This was a triumph, apparently. Weeping, with Lydia's head mashed into her chest. Oris made a note on the chart attached to Lydia's plastic bassinet, then left the room. Nathan found a tissue somewhere and wiped Edie's face.

"Can I do anything?" he asked, stroking her back.

Edie was afraid that if she moved, even to look up at him or shrug, Lydia would fall off her breast. She whispered, "No."

Nathan kissed her head again. He picked up the pile on the couch to make space to sit and saw the phone.

"Your sister called."

"What?"

He showed her: Missed call from Claudia. And below it, a text:

i'm so sorry. i lost my phone.

That's it? I'm sorry?

"Should I call her back?" asked Nathan.

"She knows where we are. She should be here with flowers. She should . . ." Lydia slipped off her breast. "Fuck! Will you please get the nurse back?"

Nathan pressed a button on the wall behind Edie's bed. Edie bent forward, a canopy over the girl, trying to drop her breast into her now-dozing daughter's slack mouth, trying to reestablish the latch. The fucking latch. She felt her back exposed in her gown. The thin sheet beneath her had bunched up. Did it even have fitted corners? How many other bare thighs had rubbed against this awful mattress? There was a knock at the door.

"Is this a good time?" asked her dad.

Edie almost laughed.

"I'm with your mom. Can we come in?"

As usual, Edie's mom was dressed all in black. Skinny jeans and chunky boots and a short leather jacket. Her bleached blond hair was pulled into a chic low ponytail. Michelle Whitehouse had been a relatively young mom, too; just twenty-three when she got pregnant with Edie while shacking up with Gabe in the London suite where he was recording with Oasis. Still, Edie had correctly suspected that her mother would be disappointed with her own early twenties pregnancy, so she'd waited until after the City Hall ceremony to break the news: Happy New Year, you're going to be grandparents! It went over like a lead zeppelin, as her dad used to say.

"You did it," said Michelle, stepping toward the bed.

Edie felt like she would never not be angry at her mother. If it weren't for her, Edie would be at home, instead of in this cold, ugly room. Instead of the rotating nurses, she would be cared for by Marianne, the doula she'd hired months ago, who was also a certified lactation consultant and massage therapist. That had been the plan until six weeks ago, when Michelle issued her ultimatum.

Edie took the train down from Poughkeepsie to meet with Jim Morgan, the man who managed the family's finances, to discuss buying a house. Michelle was born rich. Her father was a prominent Connecticut attorney before becoming a senator, and her mother's family had made a fortune in textiles for generations. They produced uniforms for the Union Army, outfitted the rangers at the National Parks system, kept the Boy Scouts in knee socks, and state prisoners around New England in stripes. The millions Edie's dad earned in the music industry added to the enormous pile, but he never felt confident managing money and let Michelle handle it all, which meant, she always said, "hiring the best people." Jim Morgan was the best. He invested for them and set Edie and Claudia up with trusts when they were babies. Jim's firm was conservative, and the money was woven into all kinds of safety nets to keep everyone and their offspring taken care of. On the day Edie was supposed to meet with Jim, her mother invited her to lunch.

It was February, but sunny, and Edie got to the Tribeca restaurant before her mother. She pointed the hostess to a table by the window in what was the back patio all summer, and transformed into a heated atrium in the winter. While she waited for her mother, Edie ordered chamomile tea and texted Nathan about the house they'd just toured. She sent him an image of a nursery she found on Pinterest and he responded with two emojis: a heart and a home. After a few minutes Michelle appeared.

"I called and reserved a table inside," she said. She was wearing four-inch-heeled ankle boots, military-style pants, and an oversized black wool coat with what Edie guessed was a fox-fur collar. As usual, her mother looked fierce. Her face just slightly flushed, her walk almost a march.

"I didn't know," said Edie. "It's nice out here."

"It's more comfortable in there. I thought you'd want to be comfortable."

"I think you and I have different ideas of what it means to be comfortable, Mom," said Edie.

"Okay, Eden," said Michelle. She sat down and when the waiter came, asked for a bottle of Pellegrino. "So, how are you?"

"I can't drink bubbles anymore." Edie rubbed her belly. "Apparently, I have acid reflux. But the baby is healthy."

"I wonder if you'll go early," said Michelle. "Claudia was

three weeks early. Which is why I wanted to meet. I gather you are still considering a home birth?"

"What do you mean considering? It's all planned."

Michelle pursed her lips and brushed her hair from her forehead with a finger. "I do not like having to do this, but if you're going to be stubborn you don't give us much choice."

"Us?"

"Your father and me."

"You're talking now?" Edie knew that her parents hadn't lived together since the fall.

"Of course we're talking. We never stopped talking. Your father and I are grown-ups, Eden. And we agree that an at-home birth is insane. I'm sorry. You will thank me. I guarantee it. You're ripped open during childbirth, for God's sake. One little nick to the wrong place and you'll bleed out before Nathan can even dial 911."

Edie cringed.

"Exactly," continued Michelle. "Everybody romanticizes having a child. But it's a horror show that first month. You're leaking everywhere. You can barely walk, and that's if you're lucky. What if the baby's breech and you have to have a C-section? Have you even thought about that?"

"Yes, we've thought of that. We see a doctor. I'm not in a cult. If the baby's breech we'll go to the hospital."

"In Poughkeepsie? Please. Why take the chance?"

"It's not Somalia," Edie said. "Babies are born there perfectly fine every day. Anyway, you can't force me to give birth where you want."

"That's true," said Michelle, "but I can make it less comfortable for you."

"What are you talking about?"

"Your father and I control your trust until you are thirty-five," she said.

"No, you don't. I got it two years ago, when I turned twenty-one."

"You got *access* to it when you were twenty-one. There is a limit on what you can withdraw before you have to have one of us approve."

"What's the limit?"

"The limit is fifty thousand."

"Since when?"

"Since always. I've tried to take some time to talk to you and Claudia both about all this, but neither of you seemed very interested. And now, I hear through Jim, that you are planning to put cash down on a house in Poughkeepsie?"

"New Paltz."

"Half a million dollars?"

"It's my money."

"And we want to make sure it stays that way."

"What are you saying?"

"There are a couple things you're going to have to do before your father and I will even consider allowing you to take that much out."

"There's, like, ten times that in there."

"Exactly. Jim has it in very smart investments. But you start whacking away at assets and the dividends go down. You girls really should learn a little more about your finances."

Edie looked at her mother. "You're telling me that I can't have *my* money to buy a house for *my* child, for *my* family, unless I give birth where you want me to give birth?"

"That, and you and Nathan need to sign a postnuptial agreement. Jim will draw it up."

"I'm not going to ask him to do that."

"Then you can keep living on your allowance and whatever you two earn until you turn thirty-five."

There wasn't much to say after that. Two weeks later, Edie and Nathan moved to Gramercy. She hadn't lived there since leaving for Vassar almost five years earlier, and instead of staying in her childhood bedroom, they set up in the guest suite on the third floor. After two days of silence, Gabe found them in the kitchen and asked for forgiveness.

"I don't agree with your mother's methods," said her father, "but the only thing that matters to me is your safety."

It was hard for Edie to stay angry at her dad. He looked terrible. Her parents talked about the separation as mutual, but it seemed clear to Edie and Claudia that their mother was the driving force. For as long as Edie could remember, Michelle had preached the value of "moving on." The girls learned quickly that, even if she was physically around to talk to, going to their mother for comfort was mostly useless. Michelle had no sympathy for those who dwelled. She'd moved past her parents' death, her youthful drug problem, and now, the father of her children. And yet, her mother managed to show up at the hospital—more, apparently, than her sister was willing to do.

"Do you want to hold her?" Edie asked her mom.

"I should wash my hands," said Michelle, looking around. "I was in a cab."

A nurse with a butch, salt-and-pepper haircut knocked.

"What do you need?" she asked.

"I can't keep her on," said Edie.

"There's a breastfeeding class in an hour," she said. "I'll come back and bring you down."

"But the other nurse said she needed to eat now."

"Never wake a sleeping baby," said the nurse.

Michelle came out of the bathroom and Edie handed Lydia to her. She looked awkward holding the girl.

"Claudia called," said Edie.

"Did you talk to her?" asked Gabe. "Where is she?"

"I missed the call, but she texted she was 'sorry.'"

"Have you girls been fighting?" asked her mom. "What happened?"

"I have no idea. She knows where we are."

"Did you call her back?" asked her dad.

"I'll send her a text," said Edie.

CLAUDIA

we have to be careful about germs the first few days but if you want to meet her you know where we are. enjoy your #staycation

Claudia supposed it was naive to have assumed Edie would forgive her for missing the birth. Should she leave a voice mail explaining what happened? *I think I dropped my phone after I got raped.* On campus there were little purple stickers in the bathrooms: *Have you been a victim of sexual assault? Tell someone.* The stickers had a phone number and a website. Confidential, they promised. And the nurse had said she trained the people on the other end of the phone. But Claudia wasn't stupid. The "counselor" at the mandatory freshman orientation was a junior: not a professional, and definitely not above gossip. *Did you hear Claudia Castro says somebody raped her?* One of those disgusting reality TV blogs that called her "the other woman" last week would probably pay ten grand for that headline.

And now Edie was against her, too. Her sister's text was ice cold. A text she'd send to a colleague: *we have to be careful about germs*. What was she saying? Was she saying Claudia was dirty? Sick? How could she know she was suddenly, possibly, both?

She considered calling her father. He hadn't actually been around any more than her mother during her childhood, but he knew how to really listen—as a music producer, that was basically his job. Claudia's parents met at a party on the Lower East Side in 1993, four years after Gabriel Castro moved three thousand miles away from Fresno to a city he'd only seen in movies. Both sides of his family had been in the San Joaquin Valley for generations: immigrants from Portugal and Armenia mixed with lapsed Mormons and Oklahoma farmers blown west by the Depression. His parents were high school sweethearts: Dad, Robert, was the only son of a widowed recruiter stationed at the naval air base in Lemoore; Mom, Brenda, grew up working the counter and measuring feet at her parents' shoe store. Vietnam called, and Robert found out Brenda was pregnant when she wrote to him at basic training. When he came home, they got married and Robert got a job as a mechanic at a private airport on the northwest side of town. But his son Freddy didn't know him and neither did Brenda—not anymore. Their marriage lasted five years; six months after Gabe turned two, Robert moved out.

The boys didn't see their dad often—he moved around, taking jobs out of state, living with roommates and sometimes in motels—but when they did, he was sober and kind and he taught Gabe how to play the guitar.

At school Gabe spent lunchtime in the music room, where he fiddled around on the piano enough that the band teacher agreed to give him formal noontime lessons. He picked up drumming and a little bit of bass. Both Castro boys were popular: They were handsome, polite, and made good grades. Freddy was the athlete—football, baseball, water polo—and Gabe the artist. He played at weddings, birthdays, and graduation parties. Junior year, he and some friends formed a band that played gigs up and down Highway 99, from Sacramento to Bakersfield. They once opened for a band that had opened for the Pixies. A guidance counselor who'd grown up in New Jersey suggested Gabe apply for scholarships back East. NYU and Boston College offered him full rides; Claudia's dad chose NYU because New York seemed like a better place for a musician.

And he was right. The school's music department had state-of-the-art studio equipment, and by the beginning of his junior year, Gabe had a meeting with Russell Simmons, who'd heard him spinning at a party in the SoHo loft of one of his wealthy classmates. For the next nine months, instead of going to class, Gabe spent his days and nights in a Greenwich Village recording studio, writing and playing and mixing and smoking weed and having the time of his life. By twenty-one Gabe had laid most of the tracks that would become his first hit record. At twenty-two the money started pouring in, and at twenty-four he had a girlfriend with a modeling contract and ancestors who had come over on the Mayflower. By twenty-seven he had two Grammys, his own SoHo loft, and a baby on the way. A town house and another daughter came a few years later; more world tours and nights in the studio and awards ceremonies and now he was a single grandfather at fifty. With Edie up in Poughkeepsie and her mom now living in an apartment in the West Village, Claudia was the only one who sometimes stayed in Gramercy with her dad—and he wasn't doing well.

Which was why Claudia decided not to call him. She needed someone steady and maybe it made no sense but the steadiest person she'd met in ages was the boy from down the hall with the cross around his neck. So she stayed inside for the next four days while the purple and red faded from her face. Trevor brought her food and they ate together and sometimes they watched something on Netflix. He was easy to talk to, just like her dad.

On Thursday, Ben texted:

will I see you saturday?

are you pissed?

i don't want to celebrate without you

As usual her ex's texts generated a range of emotions.

She felt relief: He still wants me. Annoyance: Why do I still care? And anger: If they'd been together over spring break like they'd planned she wouldn't have been hammered and wandering around the Village last Friday night. But when Ben—and apparently everyone else in the universe—saw the clip of *Rich Kids* the previous week, he got moralistic and disinvited her from the protest for immigrant rights he and some friends were going to in D.C.

"That's not the Claudia I know," he'd said sadly. They were FaceTiming, Ben in his dorm at Bard, Claudia in her Gramercy bedroom where she stayed most weekends. "I just can't believe you let them put that out there."

"I didn't *let* them," she said.

"You must have signed something."

She had, but when she walked into the party and scribbled her name she hadn't considered that there would be cameras in the fucking *bushes*. She'd had no idea she'd become a plot point.

"I didn't know," she said.

"It makes you look like a slut."

Claudia felt that word in her stomach. In her knees and her feet. Ben had managed to convince her to "open" their relationship when he left for college the year before. *We're too young to commit sexually,* he'd said. *We should explore.* He insisted it had nothing to do with love. He insisted it would strengthen their bond. They'd come back together because they wanted to, not because they had to. He held her hand as he said all this, looked into her eyes, and stroked her hair. *No one can replace you in my heart,* he said. What could she do? He gave her a book about polyamory, but it was a bunch of bullshit. What if someone saw her reading it? They were supposed to create ground rules as a couple—radical honesty, no hooking up with mutual friends—but Ben broke them all, and all they did was fight. He told her she'd understand when she got to college. He told her the "mores" were different. And now he was calling her a slut.

"Fuck you," she said.

"I said it made you *look like* a slut," said Ben, feigning hurt. Like this was all so painful for him. "Honestly, I thought you'd understand. This trip should be about the kids in cages. We don't want anything to distract from what's going on with those families."

And now he wanted her at his birthday party. Claudia put down her phone and curled up on the dorm bed. She didn't have to decide now if she would go. She could ignore him; she could run away. She could buy a plane ticket to Hawaii. Or Iceland. She could sink into hot springs, sleep under an umbrella in the humid shade. She could check into a spa in Arizona. She could take an Uber to the airport and be at the house on the Vineyard by tonight; she could walk down to the docks and feel the salt and wind in her hair. But she'd have to get out of bed. She'd have to gather up her belongings into a bag. She'd have to. Have to.

Claudia woke up a few hours later. The sun was setting and the room was lit with a hazy pink light. What had she been thinking about when she fell asleep? The reality show. She wanted to be angry, but shame felt more honest. Maybe she was a slut. And who was ever going to believe that the *Rich Kids* slut did anything but ask for it? Whatever it was. Maybe she did ask for it. Maybe she begged for it. How would she ever know? Dust motes swarmed in the stale air and Claudia suddenly felt that if she didn't escape they would poison her. They would sink into her skin and sedate her and she would fall asleep and never wake up. Sunglasses, phone, wallet, jacket, shoes. She knocked on Trevor's door and he answered.

"Wanna go on a boat ride?" she asked.

Claudia hailed a cab outside the dorm and Trevor slid in behind her.

"South Street Seaport, please," she said into the bulletproof glass. In all her years taking random ferry rides around the city, she'd never seen anyone she knew on the Circle Line. People she knew chartered boats or had their own. Claudia's mom had grown up sleeping in the cabin and diving off the bow of a fishing yacht named *Annabelle*. The boat was named after her mother's grandmother, but after Michelle's parents died in a plane crash, the lawyers sold it. Connecticut senator Owen Whitehouse and his wife, Helen, died together on Labor Day 1988. They were headed back to D.C. from Martha's Vineyard in a private plane and there was fog.

The Whitehouses left their only child, sixteen-year-old Michelle, an enormous fortune. What Claudia's mother sometimes described as "fuck-you money." And Michelle was ready to say a lot of fuck-you's. A young photographer who had seen a photo of her at the funeral reached out through the family attorney—*She'd be perfect for a fall spread I'm doing for* Vogue—and whisked her away from the sad, empty house and her suddenly tentative friends. A few months later she quit school and for the next five years, as she tells it now, Claudia's mom went hard. She never divulged details—"*way too much drugs and partying*" or, if she was in a certain mood, *"I was the definition of a hot mess"*—but sitting in the cab with the lingering sting in her eye, it occurred to Claudia that underneath those throwaway phrases were probably some horror stories. Had her mom ever woken up like she had on Saturday? How many times?

The taxi TV started its loop, too loud, with a ten-second advertisement for a Broadway show that featured people in bird costumes, their wings and feathers flapping across a stage. It was A MUST SEE! A TRIUMPH! The commercial ended and a male news anchor with a hairline as defined as a freshly poured sidewalk began to speak:

"The Subway Slasher has struck again. Police say another victim was attacked early Sunday on an F train near the Thirty-Fourth Street station. The twenty-nine-year-old male is in stable condition at Bellevue Hospital."

The picture cut to police tape and flashing lights.

"I can't believe they haven't caught him yet," said Trevor.

"Will you turn that off, please?"

"Sorry," said Trevor, pressing the screen. "It's hard to get any quiet in this city."

"That's true," said Claudia. She looked at him. "Where are you from again?"

"Ohio."

"Have you ever been out on the water?"

"No."

"It's quieter out there."

Claudia watched Trevor watch the city as they bumped and stalled their way down Bowery to the edge of the island. He was taking it all in, eyes alive; scanning and inputting sidewalks and skyscrapers and smoke shops and stoplights. He sat at attention while she slumped back.

"Are we going to the ocean?" he asked.

"Not quite. The harbor is where the East River and the Hudson meet. You have to go out pretty far to get to the actual Atlantic."

"Oh." He sounded disappointed. "I've never seen the ocean."

"Really?"

"I keep meaning to take the subway to Coney Island. That's the Atlantic Ocean, right?"

"Yeah."

"Have you ever been there?"

"To Coney Island? A couple times. The beach is a little gross."

"Oh? Some kids from my church went there for a baseball game right at the beginning of the year and said there was a whole amusement park and restaurants and stuff. Anyway, me and my roommate keep trying to go, but our schedules are kind of opposite."

"You're friends with your roommate?"

Trevor nodded. "He's different from me but he's really cool."

"You know my roommate, too, right? Whitney?"

"Yeah."

Claudia was pretty sure they were hooking up, but if he wasn't going to bring it up, she didn't need to. Not really her business. She got the sense Whitney disliked her; maybe Trevor was being polite, not passing along any gossip she'd shared in their sweaty dorm-bed sessions.

The driver let them off at Fulton Street. Claudia looked up at the board in the ticket office on Pier 6 and saw that a ninety-minute tour circling the Statue of Liberty left in fifteen minutes. She bought two tickets.

"I used to come here a lot when I was a kid," she told Trevor as they walked along the boardwalk. The scent of salt water and rotting seaweed, the squawking gulls, the wind. Did she feel a little bit better? Yes. She did. She breathed in through her nose and let her mind go backward. "Our nanny's boyfriend sold souvenirs and she used to bring us to visit him. She never wanted to actually go out on a boat, but we'd beg her and sometimes she said okay."

She and Trevor presented their tickets to the bored Circle Line employees standing at the entrance to a rope maze that led to the boat.

"You want a picture?" said one. He held a comically large camera. "It comes with."

Almost in unison Trevor and Claudia said, "No, thank you."

They walked up the clanging gangway and onto the boat. A fat tour guide was splayed in a folding chair, holding a microphone at the front of a mostly empty row of seats, talking about the currents.

A horn sounded when they got to the upper deck and the water began to churn beneath them. Claudia put her chin on the railing, its chipped green paint shiny from the grease of a million hands, and watched as the photographer on the pier lit a cigarette. He got smaller and smaller. The temperature dropped and the breeze picked up, tossing her hair across her face. She let it. Trevor said something, but she didn't catch it.

"What?" she asked.

He smiled. "I'm not sure I'd call it quiet out here."

It was true. The roar of the motor and the rush of the wind created a high-decibel ambient noise.

"You're right."

"I see what you mean, though," he shouted. "It's a different kind of loud."

The boat slowed as they passed the Statue of Liberty. On the island, tourists milled around the pedestal like ants. Trevor snapped a few photos.

"Doesn't really do it justice," he said, looking at the pictures he'd taken. "But my dad will think it's cool."

He was trying to be friendly; trying to draw her out. She should allow herself to be drawn.

"So," she said, "you go to church?"

"Yeah. Everybody at home was sure I'd get 'distracted' in New York and end up partying all the time, so my dad made me promise I'd join a church when I got here. Kind of a ready-made group of friends."

"Like a fraternity," she said.

"But coed. And they take anybody."

On the way back to the dorm, in a cab again, Claudia asked Trevor if he'd go with her to Ben's party on Saturday night. He agreed, and the next morning she realized that she didn't have a dress or pair of heels at the dorm. She Googled Prada's Spring Runway, clicked through, and found the rose-colored romper with bell sleeves she'd tried on a few weeks ago at the store on lower Broadway. Hopefully it was still in stock in her size. A few more clicks and she had two shoe options, a bag, a jacket, and three possible necklaces.

A man answered the phone at the store: *Yes, of course, Miss Castro My pleasure, Miss Castro. We'll messenger them over right away. Thank you so much.*

On Saturday night, she showered and put on the new outfit. She doubted anyone would comment on an especially heavy makeup job, and Trevor had come up with the idea to say she had an allergic reaction to mascara if anyone asked about the redness in her eye. *I can pull this off,* she thought. What could be more normal than Claudia bringing a new guy to make Ben jealous? But when Trevor showed up at her door he looked like a waiter from Chili's. Cheap plaid shirt, tan pants, and tassled loafers. Her friends were going to eat him alive.

TREVOR

A couple hours before he was supposed to meet Claudia for her ex's party, Trevor came back from the library to nap and shower. As he walked from the elevator to his room he saw a kid with a guitar strapped to his back knocking on Claudia's door.

"Hey, you know Claudia, right?" asked the kid.

"Yeah."

"Is she around?"

"I guess not if she isn't answering." Trevor had seen him on their floor but didn't know his name. "Did you text her?"

"Yeah." He looked frustrated.

"You okay?" asked Trevor.

"Your friend's kind of a bitch, dude."

Trevor narrowed his eyes, an unfamiliar, and uncomfortable, aggravation flaring inside him. "Fuck you," he said.

In the shower, he wondered what it was going to be like when everybody else came back from spring break. What was he to her? What did she need from him? Was he going to tell every dude who called her a name to fuck off? Trevor put on the best shirt and pants he had. Claudia had stressed the club had a no-sneakers policy, which didn't leave him much choice. Still, his wavy hair was cooperating, his fingernails were trimmed, his face was shaved and smooth. He even smelled good: soapy clean and just a dab of the cologne his high-school girlfriend had given him for his birthday last year. All his life he'd been told he was good-looking, and he knocked at Claudia's suite feeling confident. But when she opened the door Trevor knew he'd made a mistake agreeing to tag along. Claudia Castro was so far out of his league he might as well have been playing a different sport. She was his height now, standing in the dorm room doorway in the kind of high heels there were entire genres of porn dedicated to. Her long tan legs literally gleamed beneath a miniscule silk dress. She looked like a movie star; she practically *was* a movie star. If they hadn't literally collided in the hallway last weekend she'd have graduated without ever knowing his name.

"You look great," he said.

"Thanks." She touched her hair. "I think this is the first time I've worn a bra in a week."

Outside the dorm, Claudia hailed a cab.

"Didn't you say the party was on Ninth Street?" asked Trevor. "That's only six blocks."

"I can't really walk in these shoes," said Claudia.

Ah.

Trevor had to crane his neck to see to the top of Ben's brownstone: He counted one, two, three, four, five levels of windows, all dark, shades drawn. There was an unlit gas lantern in the little square front patio. Ivy crawled up the exterior.

"Ben's mom is kind of a hermit," said Claudia. She opened a waist-high iron gate to a just-below-street-level door and knocked. "She's always around, but she stays away."

"What about his dad?"

"He died when Ben was nine. Motorcycle accident."

Trevor's uncle had died that way when Trevor was thirteen. Uncle AJ and Trevor's dad had been riding together since they were young; dirt bikes first, then they both got Hondas in their twenties, when they could afford the insurance. Before either had wives or kids or problems. Would Claudia be interested in the story of how Trevor was pulled out of biology class to learn the news? Or that he'd spoken at the funeral? He didn't have time to find out.

"She's here!" squealed a blonde. "Where *the fuck* have you *been*? For real? I think I texted you twenty times!"

"Adrienne," said Claudia, "this is my friend Trevor."

Adrienne, her hair pulled back in ponytail so tight it took the corners of her eyes with it, looked him up and down. What did she see?

"Well, come on in, you two," she said, stepping back, sweeping an arm for them to enter. "Ben said he wasn't sure you were coming."

"I wasn't sure, either," said Claudia. "I've been sick all week."

Adrienne stepped back. "Are you contagious? You better not be contagious. You know we're going to Mauritius next week."

Claudia stiffened. "I'm fine now."

Would they believe her? It was clear to him that she was hurting, that every word she spoke took effort, but maybe the dress and make-up was enough for these people.

The room they walked into was unlike anything Trevor had ever seen in real life. He estimated you could park half a dozen cars inside. At the far end, near some sort of atrium, Trevor saw full-sized trees. He counted six sofas and three chandeliers; the walls were covered in floor-to-ceiling tapestries that looked like they belonged in a medieval castle. The whole place had a citadel vibe: a suit of armor in one corner faced a life-sized horse constructed of what he guessed was driftwood in another. And above him, a second blonde, this one with her long hair hanging loose past her shoulders, stood on an interior stone balcony. A Juliet balcony, Trevor knew from years building sets for the community theater where his mom worked. He'd planned to hook up with the theater world at NYU, but the first show he volunteered for required a twenty-hour weekly commitment, and he had to bail at the end of September because he was so behind in classwork. The amount of reading alone was easily five times what he'd ever been given in high school. Even his roommate Boyd agreed that it was literally impossible to read everything the professors assigned. The difference was that Boyd, who had attended a private boarding school in Connecticut, seemed used to it, while Trevor was struggling. So no more extracurriculars except church. And no spring break. Unless you counted Claudia.

The girl on the balcony appeared to be taking a selfie. She shook out her hair, then leaned over the railing.

"Has anybody ever spit on you, Ben?" she shouted.

The ex, Ben, was rolling a joint on a leather sofa worn light and soft with age, but probably still worth more than any car Trevor's family had ever owned.

"No, Lolly," said Ben, not lifting his head. "No one has ever spit on me in my own house."

Lolly laughed and cleared her throat like she was about to hock a loogie from the balcony.

"You're disgusting, Lolly," shouted a lanky redhead standing behind the bar, which appeared to be fashioned from a single slice of some massive tree. The redhead was dressed in a paisley shirt, open to reveal chest hair, and plunking oversized ice cubes into crystal glasses with a pair of tongs.

"You're a loser, Harris," shouted Lolly. Then: "Claudia!"

Trevor watched Ben see Claudia. Watched his face brighten into a smile. Fuck, he thought. I'm going back to the dorm alone.

"Come on, pretty lady," said Ben. "First puff is yours."

Claudia went to him. She sat down and inhaled and let him stroke her hair.

"You all good?" he asked.

She looked at Ben and for a moment Trevor thought she was going to kiss him. He felt his heart shudder. But then her face reset. Claudia nodded, sucked on the joint a second time, and looked up at Trevor. "You want?"

"I'm good," he said. He hadn't smoked since getting arrested and tonight didn't seem like the night to restart.

"Who's your friend, Claudia?" asked Lolly, descending the winding stone staircase from the balcony. Her dress looked like it was made from Kleenex and her feet were bare. Lolly put her hand on Trevor's shoulder, let her fingers slide down to his elbow. He looked at Claudia and stiffened, but she didn't seem to care.

"This is Trevor," Claudia said.

"You go to NYU?" asked Lolly. "What are you studying?" Before he could answer, Lolly continued. "I really hope you don't say business. Every fucking guy I meet says he's studying business. Come on! Doesn't anybody study art anymore? Or history? Or fucking literature?" She punctuated each syllable of the final word with a faux British flourish.

Ben chuckled.

"*Because*," said Adrienne, "you can't make money in art or history or fucking literature. We've been arguing about this. My sister has decided she wants to marry an artist."

"Not *marry*. And not just an artist. Somebody who can, like, build stuff. Like, an *installation* artist. You know that guy I was dating, the one from Geneva? He literally couldn't rehang a picture that fell off the wall at his apartment. He called the super."

"You broke up with him over that?" said Ben. "You ladies are cold."

"He broke up with her," said Adrienne.

"It was mutual," said Lolly. "*Anyway*, back to the point. Which is that a man should have practical skills. He should be able to build things."

"What do you need built, Lolly?" asked Harris.

"Nothing!"

"We get it, love," said Ben. "You want a real man."

"Exactly. A real man."

"Trevor, do you want a beer?" asked Harris

"Sure," said Trevor.

"At your service!" Harris saluted, pulled a tall glass from the wall of stemware behind him, then bent down and brought up a bottle of beer and poured slowly. "I'm working on the foam issue."

"Harris likes playing bartender," said Lolly. She turned to Trevor. "So where are you from, Trevor?"

"Ohio."

"Shut up," said Adrienne, pulling out her phone. "What's your Insta?"

He told her and she searched him. He'd only posted three times since leaving home: an NYU banner; a selfie with his three suitemates; hippie musicians playing beneath the arch in Washington Square Park. The rest of his feed was high school. Church and dances and track meets and cast parties and camping. After a few seconds of scrolling, Adrienne turned her phone around and shoved it toward her sister's face.

"Oh my God, he was Homecoming King?!"

Lolly plopped down on the sofa and patted the seat next to her. "Come sit, King Trevor. Tell me more about yourself."

"I'm studying business."

"No!" Lolly squealed, simultaneously feigning disappointment and delight. Ben nodded his head, amused. Even Claudia smiled.

"Is that true?" Claudia asked.

"No," he said.

"OMG, you're awesome. This guy is hilarious, Claudia."

There was a knock at the door and Adrienne flitted away to answer.

"Who else is coming?" asked Harris as he handed Trevor the beer.

"I told everybody they could come by or meet us at the club," said Ben. "The set starts at eleven and I've got Ubers coming at ten thirty."

Adrienne squealed at the door and Lolly went to see who it was. Trevor drank his beer and asked Harris for another. Over the next hour, half a dozen more people entered the house. Everyone was up and hugging, dropping purses, finding drinks, taking selfies, sending messages. Ben opened a box that looked like a chess set but inside were weed vapes: "Party favors," he announced, and passed them around. Harris shattered a wine glass, prompting applause. Finally Ben whistled—an impressive, practiced call—and it was time to get into the Ubers.

On the sidewalk, just as they were about to climb into the SUV, Claudia grabbed Trevor's hand and said, "I'm so glad you're here."

She looked him right in the eye. He thought: *She needs me.* And though he knew it was not the same thing, he allowed his mind to think—to hope: *She wants me.* Lolly and Adrienne got in the far back seat with another girl whose name Trevor didn't catch, and Claudia and Trevor sat next to each other in the middle row. The nameless girl pulled out a Juul and started to puff. In the rearview mirror, Trevor could see the driver watching her. But he didn't say anything.

"Did you tell Claudia you invited Chad?" Adrienne asked Lolly.

"I invited Chad," said Lolly. "I saw him yesterday at the gym. I figured you guys were cool again after Friday."

"Friday?" asked Claudia.

"When we left Down Under you two were hanging out."

"Oh, right. Yeah, cool."

Trevor looked at Claudia. She seemed to be concentrating really hard. Down Under was a foul-smelling bar near campus that was known for a loose ID policy. Trevor had been there once with Boyd, but they'd left after a drunk guy called Boyd a faggot.

"Who's Chad?" asked the nameless girl.

"We went to school with him for a while," said Adrienne. "Then he moved to L.A."

"Why would Claudia care if he's coming?"

"I don't care," said Claudia.

"They had a little thing in high school and she dumped him for Ben and he got all upset."

"Is that what happened?" asked Lolly.

"It doesn't matter," said Claudia. "It was a long time ago."

"Right," said Adrienne. "And you're cool now. Like I said. He goes to NYU, too, right?"

"Right," said Claudia. "He's in my dorm."

They pulled up to the club and Trevor let the girls get out first. It was the kind of place he'd seen on TV: a long velvet rope with people lined up waiting to get in; big men with walkie-talkies and clipboards standing guard; red light bleeding from inside each time the heavy entrance doors opened.

Lolly and Adrienne walked to the front and the rope parted for them all. A tall woman in a sparkly black dress and sandals that buckled up her calves showed them to an elevated corner-booth area. The table at their ankles was crowded with half a dozen bottles of liquor and glass carafes of what he assumed were cranberry juice and orange juice. Perrier. Ice in a silver bucket. Harris went to work, kneeling down, pouring, passing. The music was too loud and the lights were too low. Everybody seemed to move back and forth between behaving as if they were on display and entirely alone. Adrienne stood at the railing separating their sofas from the main dance floor, posing with her lips around her cocktail straw as she surveyed the room, assessing. Trevor watched as she stirred her drink, then stuck her thumb in her nose, pinched something out, and let it fall from her fingers to the floor.

Claudia was at the railing, too, facing the crowd but not examining with Adrienne's purpose. It was as if she were looking at the ocean.

"You okay?" he asked her.

She nodded. "Are you having fun?"

"Yeah," he said.

"Good. Thanks for coming."

"Thanks for inviting me."

"Lolly wants to hook up with you," Claudia said. "You should if you want. Not that you need my permission. She's cool. She does the whole Earth Mother thing. She loves nice guys."

What could he say? "Well, that's me."

At least that made her smile.

"Drink?" shouted Ben, holding a glass, motioning to Trevor.

"I'm going to the bathroom," said Claudia.

Trevor took the glass from Ben and sat down.

"Happy birthday," Trevor said. "It's a big one."

"I kind of can't believe I'm spending my twenty-first doing the same shit we've been doing for years. This fucking club. Yawn. Don't tell these guys I said that."

"I won't."

"I should be jumping out of an airplane or something."

"I did that once."

"You did? What was it like?"

"It was amazing," said Trevor. He'd gone with his youth group for graduation. "Like flying."

"See? Exactly." He leaned back and shook his head. "I guess I gotta start taking shit in hand."

Trevor and Ben watched the crowd from the booth. More people joined them, but no one else introduced themselves to Trevor. Claudia came back from the bathroom and poured herself a drink, drank it quickly, poured another, and then stood up abruptly, knocking into a newcomer. She fell forward, hitting the table with her hip, toppling what was left of the cranberry juice into the ice bucket, and the ice bucket onto the floor.

"Castro's drunk already," said the guy she'd bumped into, laughing.

Claudia sat for a moment on the floor, her feet angled awkwardly beside her. Ben remained on the sofa. Trevor reached forward. "You okay?"

She took his hand and stood up, grabbed the railing, then let go and disappeared down into the dance floor.

Adrienne and the nameless girl from the car laughed and rolled their eyes.

"Nice going, Chad," said Ben.

Chad sat down beside Trevor, leaning in toward what was left of the liquor tray.

"That girl needs to slow *down*," he said, pouring a drink. "For real. Is there anybody at this party who hasn't fucked her?"

"Whoa," said Trevor.

"Who are you?" asked Chad.

"This is Trevor," said Ben. "He's with Claudia."

Chad stopped pouring and looked at Trevor. "You better use protection, dude. For real."

Nameless giggled.

"I thought you guys were her friends," said Trevor, and maybe his tone was a little accusatory. But come on. Her ex was just going to let this guy talk like that?

"That's the problem," muttered Ben, motioning to the waitress to take care of Claudia's spill.

"What's the problem, Ben?" asked Chad, his voice rising.

"That you guys are friends. Just friends."

"Fuck you."

"Fuck *you*," said Ben. "Seriously, why are you here? It's not his fault you can't close a deal you've been working on for five years. Did you think it was gonna happen tonight?"

"I wouldn't touch that shit with a *pole*, man. She fucked a guy in our dorm the first *week* at school. Did her whole,

I'm-so-into-you-thing, then dropped him cold. Gave him *crabs.* I'm serious. He was pissed."

Trevor stood up, maybe a little too close to Chad.

"Whoa," said Chad, looking up. "I'm just trying to give you the heads-up, buddy."

"I'm not your buddy," said Trevor.

TREVOR

They shared a cab back to the dorm in silence. Claudia held Trevor's elbow getting in, then she shut her eyes and leaned her forehead on the window. How drunk was she? How drunk was he? The club's music buzzed in his ears, a pressing, insistent residue of the night. His body was awash in intoxicants; alcohol, sugar, nicotine, envy, anger, arousal.

Claudia let herself into her room and before she closed the door she whispered, "Thank you." And then: "I'm sorry." And then, again: "Thank you."

The video popped up on Trevor's phone the next evening. He was getting his backpack ready for Bible study when it came in as a text from a blocked number, sent at 5:37 p.m.

Claudia Castro is a whore

He pressed play, not really even thinking. The image was a close-up so extreme it took a moment for him to recognize what he was looking at. A woman's mouth. Pubic hair. An erect penis. The camera pulled back and he saw that the woman was Claudia. Her eyes were closed, her hair obscuring much of her face. She was on her hands and knees and there was a guy in a gray T-shirt behind her. It was the kid he'd seen outside her door. The one with the guitar. Trevor heard the muted, rough sounds of bodies moving against each other. Then a voice: "Dude, she peed!" The camera swung around and there was Chad, the asshole from Ben's party. He was bare chested, his face red and sweaty and smiling.

The first thing Trevor thought was, *I have to show her this.* And then, *I can't show her this.* And then, *I have to show this to somebody.* And then, *I can't show this to anybody.*

Five minutes later, Claudia knocked at his door. He saw in her face that whoever had sent it to him had sent it to her, too. And something about the way he looked must have told her the same. She walked in, sat on his sofa, and put her head in her hands. The sun was setting between two of the NYU housing towers outside his window, casting the cluttered room with a dramatic glow.

"I wonder if he sent it to anyone else," Claudia whispered. "I wonder if it's online."

"Do you want me to check?"

She didn't respond.

"Was that last Friday night?" he asked.

"I was really drunk."

He wanted to say, *I love you.* He wanted to say, *They will pay for this.*

She noticed his backpack by the door. "Where are you going?"

"Church," he said. A pause. "Wanna come?"

The door to Pastor Evan's apartment was propped open with a woman's shoe. A dainty sneaker, bleached white. Inside there was laughing. Whitney's laugh was most prominent, as usual. Whitney laughed a lot, and until that moment standing at the door with Claudia, Trevor had thought her boisterousness attractive. Not anymore. Her laugh was an affront now. Like a waving flag of ignorance. This was going to end badly. Trevor grabbed Claudia's hand and turned to leave, but Whitney was too quick, bounding from inside the apartment to wrap her arms around his neck.

"Trevor!"

He endured her hug, and then Whitney stiffened when she saw Claudia behind him.

"What are you doing here?" she asked, not even trying to hide her displeasure.

"I asked her to come," said Trevor.

Before Whitney could continue her questions, someone hollered from the kitchen: "Trev! Where's the pizza? I'm starving!"

Shit. He'd been on the schedule to bring pizza this week and he'd forgotten. If Claudia hadn't been with him, if he hadn't felt the need to protect her from Whitney, he would have made a joke about being a bonehead, but he just stood there. Pastor Evan's wife, Andrea, rescued him.

"I'll call," she said, pulling out her phone. "We can get started."

Around her, the dozen or so people gathered for the Sunday evening session started choosing seats: on the sofa, the IKEA coffee table that doubled as a bench, the kitchen chairs, pillows on the floor.

"I'm Andrea," she said, extending her hand to Claudia. "Welcome."

"Thanks," said Claudia. She sat down next to Trevor on the rug. Pastor Evan asked everyone to hold hands and Claudia went along with it, even bowing her head when they started to pray. Trevor felt deeply embarrassed by the earnest rituals. What good would all this do her? Claudia didn't need forgiveness. He didn't know what she needed, but he knew she wasn't going to find it here.

CLAUDIA

If she'd been able to form a coherent thought at all, she would have said no thanks when Trevor invited her to church. Church! In an apartment! And her fucking roommate from Texas giving her the side-eye the whole time. She made herself stay put through the pastor's little sermon and then bolted down the stairs and walked toward Washington Square Park. It was the warmest evening yet this spring, the sky still blue but the streets and buildings darkening. A month ago she would have thought the temperature hopeful: Summer! The Vineyard. The beach and the boys and riding her bike along the flat paths. Legs pumping against the wind. But hopeful was not a description she could imagine giving to anything now. Hopeful had been fried.

Who else had seen Chad's video? It could be a thousand

people by now. And how would she know? Would anybody call her up and say, *Claudia, there's a video of you getting double-teamed on Snapchat. You might want to, like, call somebody about getting it taken down.* Her head was bowed, hair obscuring her face for most of the fifty-eight seconds, so you'd have to freeze that one frame to know it was her. But if you did, you'd know. And it was never going to go away. It would live in the cloud or the wires or whatever the Internet actually was until the end of time. Anyone with high school hacking abilities could pull it up in five minutes. For the rest of her life she was going to have to assume that every person she met had seen her with a dick in her mouth. For the rest of her life she was going to see that look she saw on Trevor's face when she knocked on his door. Pity and scorn and lust and revulsion. That was how she would be greeted for the rest of her life. And all because she'd agreed to go to the movies with Chad fucking Drake four years ago.

If she hadn't said yes they would never have held hands. And if they had never held hands he wouldn't have had a reason to hate her.

She could blame Edie, if she thought about it a certain way. If her sister hadn't slept with Chad's epically slimy dad, Ridley, Claudia and Chad would probably just have remained acquaintances. Students at the same school, occasionally seeing each other on the beach or at the ice cream shop or at a party on the Vineyard, where both their families had homes. For years, Claudia Castro and Chad Drake had been in the same rooms together, but she never found him especially attractive or interesting. He seemed to talk almost exclusively about sports. Then, all of a sudden, they had something in common.

It was Memorial Day weekend and the annual Edgartown yacht club opening party. She had just turned fifteen and Edie was off to college in the fall. Claudia was standing by the railing of the club's deck, staring at her sister and Ridley flirting in a corner they probably thought was private, when Chad came up to her.

"He can do it in the open now," said Chad. "They're officially getting a divorce."

Chad was almost a foot taller than she was and when she turned to look at him she noticed his jaw was red with razor rash. Edie had commented on the bumps along Claudia's bikini line just that morning, and she remembered thinking it must really suck to deal with that on your face.

"I'm sorry," she said. She was embarrassed by her sister's behavior. Claudia was barely in high school and even she'd heard the rumors about Ridley Drake. Was her sister really that dumb? That desperate for attention?

"*I'm* sorry," said Chad. "Is Edie even eighteen yet?"

Claudia nodded. "I don't get it. He's older than our dad."

"Women are attracted to power," he said.

"That's such a cliché." Maybe, she thought, if her parents hadn't spent half of Claudia and Edie's childhood on tour, leaving them for weeks every other month in the care of nannies and housekeepers, Edie wouldn't find the affections of a man twice her age quite so exciting. Daddy issues. Nothing was more cliché than that.

"Cliché is just a shitty kind of true, though, right?" said Chad.

"I guess. That's a weird way to think about it."

"The whole thing is weird."

It got even weirder when Edie got pregnant. Ridley connected Claudia's sister to a doctor in Manhattan, paid for the procedure, and dispensed with her by Labor Day. In the years since, Claudia wondered whether Chad would have gotten so fierce about everything if what he'd had was just a regular crush, instead of a crush complicated by Edie and Ridley's sordid backstory. The crush—was it mutual?—became apparent as soon as they returned to school that fall and were partnered in biology class. Now they had lots to talk about and none of it involved their awkward family connection. But that part of the connection was always in the background. They began building a friendship around shared humor and intelligence and a little bit of teenage chemistry, but the foundation was rotten. It stank the whole time.

Almost from the beginning, Claudia sensed that Chad liked her in a way no other boy had yet, and it both frightened and excited her. She'd been French kissed, but the experiences were largely unpleasant experiments of saliva and tongue. She never knew where to put her hands, and she never felt anything below her chin. Until Chad. It came on suddenly. For months they cracked each other up as bio partners, stifling giggles and passing notes about asexual reproduction, studying occasionally at each other's apartments, and texting late into the night. It was time of transition with her female friends, boyfriends starting to fill up conversations and weekends. What could she contribute to a discussion about sex when you're on your period, or whether to wrap your lips over your teeth when you're giving a blowjob? Nothing. So she found herself hanging out with Chad and his jock friends more often. Talking about music and school and even finding herself mildly interested in some of the details about who got traded and who got upset in the various sports they all followed. She didn't know that Chad always left the party soon after she did. And she didn't know, although she suspected, that they teased him about how much he liked her. Why shouldn't she enjoy his attention? What could it possibly hurt?

That April, the Castros went to Mexico with another family for spring break. While she was there, Claudia made out with another feel-nothing boy on the beach and when she got back to bed in the room she and Edie shared, she imagined kissing Chad. She buried herself beneath the sheets in the dark and closed her eyes and stayed awake for an hour marveling at, enjoying, the way her body was suddenly warm. She felt slinky. She felt, for the first time, sexy. She'd had a crush on Ben—then a sophomore in her studio art class—all year, but he hadn't yet show any interest. So, while she could moon over him, the understanding that Chad actively wanted to do things with her made daydreaming about him more potent; she had the power to make it real.

Unfortunately, the Chad in her Mexico fantasy was not the Chad in bio class. The Chad in bio class had more than mild acne and his ears stuck out and he bit his nails down to gross little crescent moons. Still, she liked being with him, so when he asked her to go see *Trainwreck* together she said sure. And when their fingers ended up intertwined forty minutes through the movie, she thought maybe she could get past the cringeworthy details of his appearance and his clumsy manner. She was ready for a boyfriend. Ready to do the things her friends were talking about doing, ready to enter that grown-up world of skin and dark and wet.

But when she saw Chad at school on the Monday after the movies, she knew it wasn't going to happen. She didn't want to kiss him. In fact, the idea made her feel a little bit sick. Instead of meeting him before biology at her locker, she dawdled in the bathroom, then avoided eye contact by sneaking in just as the bell rang. After class, she bolted back to the bathroom. They usually saw each other again at lunch, sitting with one of their rotating groups on the benches in the school courtyard, or across the street at the deli. But Claudia left the building out a side door and when he texted if she wanted to meet up later, she didn't text back. Should she have just had the awkward conversation with him? Yes, obviously. And, obviously, she shouldn't have been surprised when he started a rumor that he'd seen her give a blow job to a junior from another school at a party. Or, after that, when the friends they shared shunned her. But she was, a little. It seemed like asymmetrical punishment. The furthest she'd gone with a guy was getting felt up in the back of an Uber, and now her classmates were tagging her on Snapchat stories of "famous sluts." Cleopatra; Angelina Jolie; Kim Kardashian; Claudia Castro. Fine. She endured, and that summer Chad went to California to stay with his mom; he finished the rest of high school in L.A. His friends were still assholes to her, but by the middle of junior year she was with Ben, so she didn't care.

She and Chad had un-followed each other on social media by the time he left New York, so it was a legitimate shock that August when, almost three years later, he plopped down on the couch next to her at the dorm orientation. He'd come back to the city for college. He smiled at her, and she let it all go. Claudia was done with Ben and his polyamory pretext; she was ready to start college looking forward, not back. She wasn't the person she'd been when she'd embarrassed Chad. She'd changed, and maybe Chad had, too. Maybe he was ready to forgive her. If Chad Drake could be her friend again, she figured, anything was possible.

"You ready for all this?" Chad asked, as the counselors droned on about academic integrity and coping with stress.

"All this?"

He gestured to the room. "Living in a dorm. Hanging out with people from, like, Ohio."

"Are you?"

"I'm ready to leave all that shit from high school *behind.* I'm diving in."

"Me, too."

He said he was thinking about studying business, or maybe political science. His dad, of course, wanted him to go to law school.

"Did either of your parents get remarried?" Claudia asked.

"My mom's got a boyfriend."

"What about your dad?"

"He's still an asshole."

The day before, if someone had asked her to describe Chad, she might have used the same word. But this Chad was talking to her. He wasn't recoiling at her very presence. And it was easy to remember why she'd liked him in the first place.

After the orientation, she and Chad joined a group headed to a pho restaurant that didn't card. Around ten, Claudia paid her share of the bill and got up from the table. Chad stopped her at the door.

"Hey," he said quietly. "I'm really sorry."

"Thanks," she said. "Me, too."

"I just liked you so much."

It was the nicest thing she'd heard in months. So she kissed him. But when he texted asking if she wanted to hang out the next day, she texted back that she had plans: *i'm sure i'll see u around!*

A couple days later, she kissed Jeremy from Long Island. They'd been on line to buy textbooks. Everyone around them was wearing a T-shirt that announced some aspect of themselves—FEMINIST; NYU VOLLEYBALL; NICE STORY, BRO—but Jeremy was wearing a faded plaid button-up and jeans that fit just right. He had short brown hair and blue eyes and the new Claudia was ready to start life as a sexually active single woman. Being with Ben had taught her how to get pleasure, and if she couldn't be fooling around with Ben, she wanted to be fooling around. Because fooling around was fun. She was on the Pill and she'd insist on condoms, of course. She'd promised herself she wouldn't have sex unless she wanted to. And she wanted to.

"Where you going after this?" Jeremy asked. It was six thirty, and she didn't have plans until nine. "I've got pot," he said. "Wanna go to the park?"

They made out on a bench next to the playground. Somebody walked by and muttered, "Get a room." In response, Jeremy slipped his hand under her shirt. She loved it. Jeremy told her he was in a band and they were recording at a studio on Bleecker later that night. He said he was studying classical guitar, but liked making all kinds of music. Music, he said, was his life. He asked her if she was into music and she almost laughed—should she tell him who her dad was? But she didn't want to seem like a bitch. She was working on that. As the sun started to go down and the performers by the water fountain changed shifts, Jeremy asked for her number and she gave it to him. But she didn't program his name into her phone; if he texted after that, she probably missed it.

So, Claudia wasn't thinking about Jeremy or Chad when she walked into Down Under with Lolly and Adrienne last Friday night. The three of them had shared a joint before treating themselves to the tasting menu—plus wine pairings—at a new SoHo restaurant. They giggled and pranced north into the Village, and when they passed the revelers spilling out of the bar Lolly announced that the irony of starting the evening at a Michelin-starred restaurant and ending it at a notorious dive was too perfect to ignore. To the extent that she could think straight at all, Claudia was thinking about Ben, and what he'd called her. She was thinking about all the strangers online who'd seen the stupid TV show and were calling her the same thing. She was thinking that everybody makes mistakes when they're eighteen and wasn't it just her shit luck that hers got captured for the whole world to see. But she wasn't going to let Ben or a crappy reality show ruin her life. She was in the greatest city in the world and she was on spring break.

Had Chad and Jeremy known each other before that night? Did she try to fight? Was that how she'd gotten hurt? Or was hitting her in the face part of the fun? And who was going to believe her when she said she'd been wronged? Please. She was a drunk rich girl. There was probably video of her leaving the bar with both of them. She'd probably been laughing.

After leaving Trevor in the pastor's apartment, Claudia paced the paths in the park for what felt like hours. What was going to happen next? Near the new playground, she saw a group of kids from her dorm and quickly turned away, scrambling to shove her earbuds in so she could pretend not to hear if someone called her name. She didn't want to leave the park until she had a plan. But as evening turned to night, as the moms pushing strollers were replaced with people dragging shopping carts, she became more and more agitated. All around her men were looking at women, talking to women, touching women. What had those men done the night before? What didn't those women know about them? She wanted to grab every girl she saw: *Don't trust him*, she'd warn. *It's getting dark and you can't possibly know what he is, what he's done, what he'll do.* She saw herself running and screaming through the park, pushing people apart, interrupting picnics and photo sessions below the arch. Someone would get a picture of her and sell it to the *Post.* "CLAUDIA CASTRO GOES CRAZY!"

At the corner of the park and West Fourth, someone touched her shoulder. She looked up, and there was Daphne Daniels, from her art history section. And beside her, Jeremy.

"Hey," said Daphne, smiling. "How was your break?"

"Fine."

"Mine went *so* fast."

Claudia did not respond.

"Jeremy, do you know Claudia?"

"Sure," said Jeremy, hiking up the guitar case on his shoulder. "Everybody knows Claudia Castro."

Daphne giggled. *Oh, God,* thought Claudia, *she likes him.* Jeremy smiled at Claudia, smiled at Daphne. Winked. Claudia didn't lunge at him. But she thought about it.

"Did you end up going anywhere?" he asked her.

Claudia's stomach started to cramp. Had she talked about her broken plans? Had she mentioned Ben? *Why was he smiling?* She shook her head.

"Okay. I'm off. See you ladies later." He walked backward a few steps, grinning at them both, his arms positioned as if he were playing a guitar. "Practice time," he said, twiddling his fingers dramatically.

"He's not my usual type, but I think he's really cute," said Daphne. Claudia focused on the streetlight. The red hand blinking, the crosswalk countdown clock: 10, 9, 8, 7 . . .

"Are you okay?" asked Daphne.

"What?"

"You look a little sick."

Claudia bent forward and vomited onto the sidewalk. Daphne jumped back. Claudia vomited again. Tears leaked from her eyes and she felt the wet splatter on her ankles. Her face had healed but what Jeremy and Chad did had infected her. She was different now, and they were the same.

PART 2

ONE WEEK LATER

EDIE

"I wanted your sister to be here but she isn't answering my texts," said Michelle.

"I haven't heard from her either," said Edie.

"I'm sure she feels terrible about missing the birth. She probably needs you to take the lead."

Edie and her mom were sitting in the living area on the main floor of the family's Gramercy Park town house. The whole level was one large room: a sitting area with sofas and armchairs, area rugs, and small tables facing a rarely used—but always ready—fireplace. One long, white-painted brick wall connected to the dining area and kitchen, with its marble island and countertops, cut-glass cabinets, and tub-sized farm sink, and then to the double-height sunroom that opened to the back garden. The family's housekeeper, Olena, who'd been coming in the morning and leaving in the evening five days a week since Edie and Claudia were in elementary school, was upstairs making beds.

The last time Edie had been in this room with her mother was just before Christmas, when her parents announced they were separating.

"We love each other, but we want different kinds of lives," Michelle had said. "You girls are grown now. You don't really need us."

"Since when has that mattered?" Edie asked, and immediately regretted it. She didn't want to start a fight. Since getting pregnant, Edie had been thinking a lot about her upbringing. She found a therapist in New Paltz and drove there every week to work out how she wanted to raise her own child differently. The therapist called Michelle and Gabe's parenting style "benign neglect," and suggested that the roots that should connect the four of them were shallow, the connections untended, which made facing challenges together difficult. What Edie had wanted to say to her mother in that moment was something like, *We needed you more—we still need you.* Was it the shallow roots that turned what felt like a plea on the inside into meanness when it hit the air? "I just never got the sense that our needs figured much into your plans."

"I'm sorry, Eden," said Michelle. "Are you complaining about the freedoms we allowed you? You certainly seemed to enjoy them at the time. And look at you. A Seven Sisters graduate, Claudia at NYU. I didn't go to college, and your dad never graduated. You girls had everything. *Have* everything. But somehow we didn't meet your needs as parents?"

"I don't think that's what she means, Mom," said Claudia, trying to manage the situation. Claudia, who didn't get her feelings hurt. But Michelle interrupted.

"I am forty-seven years old. My parents were both dead at fifty. I chose your dad because I loved him and I wanted to live my life with him. And we lived a great life together. We raised you—whether you like how we did it or not. But things change. People change. Your father has his music. That's enough for him. He doesn't need me anymore, either."

The sisters looked at their dad, standing half a room away, gripping the back of one of the tall chairs at the kitchen island.

"Dad?" asked Claudia.

Gabe looked at Michelle and then his daughters. There was no fight in him. Edie touched her belly and said silently to the still-secret, plum-sized baby inside: *I will never run out of fight for you.*

"Your mom's made up her mind," said Gabe.

Michelle stood up abruptly: "Fine, make me the bad guy."

Did she really not understand that she was blowing up their world? They were a family, and now she wanted out.

Upstairs, Edie and Claudia cried together, and Edie told her sister about the pregnancy. But Claudia didn't react the way Edie had hoped. She started ranting about their mom, and how she couldn't even manage to teach her daughters how to use birth control, and that she couldn't believe she'd ever looked up to her, ever thought her superficial life was something to aspire to. *We should know better*, Claudia kept saying. *We should know better.*

Edie tried to recall: How long had it been since she'd

texted Claudia? Day and night ran together in a series of three-hour loops: feed then burp then diaper then swaddle then an hour of sleep, maybe two, then start again. Gabe traded shifts with Nathan, rocking and changing, but Edie was the only one who could feed Lydia. Unless they gave up and switched to formula. That's how the pediatrician put it. *A lot of women give up these days.* And the lactation consultant, too: *Don't give up! I know you can do it!* They'd just said goodbye to the consultant when Michelle came by with her urgent news that had to be delivered in person. Nathan was at the kitchen island clicking away on the laptop, trying to get same-day delivery of all the things the woman recommended: pads and pump and pillow, supplements, swaddle, noise machine, night light. Lydia, exhausted from the fight to eat, was asleep in the bassinet. They'd been to the pediatrician twice and the little girl was underweight. Hours and hours, days in the new rocking chair, or propped up against the headboard, bent over with her daughter sucking, and it wasn't enough. She shouldn't have done this. Her body was telling her she shouldn't have done this.

And now here came her mom with news that apparently required another sit-down.

"Like I said, I was hoping Claudia would be here, too," said Michelle. "But she hasn't answered. I've already talked to your father." She paused. "I've been seeing someone. Casually. But, apparently, we've been photographed together, and the *Post* is going to run an item. Probably tomorrow."

"An item?"

"It's ridiculous. Obviously, a slow news week. But there's

nothing we can do about it. Which is why I'm telling you. I really don't mean to upset you right now. I know this is tough."

"Do you?"

"I don't want to fight, Eden. I know this isn't what you wanted. But it's not so bad, is it? And I know that lactation woman probably gave you a whole bunch of guilt shit, but you don't have to breastfeed. Lydia will be just fine either way."

"Everybody breastfeeds."

"That's not true."

"If you can breastfeed, I can breastfeed."

"I didn't breastfeed."

"Yes, you did."

"No, I didn't."

"You told us you did."

"I lied," said her mom. "It was hard and I was lazy and I gave up. I wanted you to think I'd done it. I wanted to have done it."

Edie almost laughed. "You lied about breastfeeding?"

Michelle shrugged. "It's not my proudest moment. I'm coming clean now."

"Does Claudia know?"

"About me and Ridley?"

Edie's heart jumped. "What?"

"Oh, you mean about breastfeeding? I doubt it."

"Ridley?"

"Ridley Drake. The man I'm seeing. You remember him. His son, Chad, went to school with Claudia."

This isn't real, thought Edie. She looked at her mother.

She looked at Nathan. He knew that name; she'd told him everything.

"Like I said, it's not serious," continued Michelle. "We've known each other a long time. He grew up in Greenwich, too."

It was real. What should she say? The summer Ridley got her pregnant Edie's parents were still running around the world on tour, and as far as she knew, they had no idea what had happened between them. She needed to talk to Claudia. Now.

"He's a *dick*, Mom."

"Excuse me?"

Edie wanted to say, *He sleeps with teenagers*. But instead she just muttered, "He's so sleazy."

"I don't expect you to approve," she said. "And obviously this is not how I wanted you and Claudia to find out."

"What about Dad?"

"What about him?"

"Does he know?"

"Yes. I told you he did." Edie's body felt like it was melting into the sofa, but her mom stood, unburdened now, ready to wrap up the conversation. "I just wanted you to know in case you see anything online. Like I said, it must be a very slow news week. Anyway, can I get you anything? Do you have bottles? I'd love to feed her when she wakes up. You two can get some rest. Take a walk, even. It's beautiful out."

"We're fine, Mom." Edie couldn't look up.

"Okay. I've talked to your father and I'm going to stay here for a couple nights. I don't want to feed this Ridley thing.

You know how this stuff goes. If they can snap a few more pictures it'll live longer, but if we lay low they'll move on."

We. Her mother and Ridley Drake were a *we*.

When Michelle finally went upstairs, Nathan closed his laptop and sat next to Edie.

"What can I do?" he asked.

"I can't believe he's fucking my mom," said Edie. "That's . . . insane. I need to talk to Claudia."

She asked Nathan to find her phone and when she scrolled into her messages she saw it had been nearly two weeks since she'd sent the text to Claudia. Edie started typing: *I'm sorry for the bitchy text. I love you. We need to talk! You need to meet your niece! Call me! Come to the house!*

Lydia started whimpering in her bassinet. The sound sent chills up Edie's spine. Nathan put his hand on the girl, wrapped like a papoose in a thick cotton blanket. *Shhhh*, he whispered. *Shhhh*. The baby quieted. *What kind of person recoils from the sounds her child makes?* Edie was supposed to be happy, but mostly she felt burdened. And now her mother had brought Ridley Drake into her life again.

"Claudia is going to freak out." Though it was Edie who'd gotten pregnant and dumped, Claudia was the one who was most outraged by Ridley's behavior. Edie was so besotted she would have done anything to get him back, but Claudia saw the whole thing for what it was: a vain, careless man playing with a pretty toy, who just happened to be a human being. Edie had been surprised when Claudia got friendly with Ridley's son, Chad, but Claudia assured her Chad hated his dad as much as they did. *We make fun of him*, she remembers Claudia telling her over the phone that dark first year at Vassar when her roommate was a virgin from Arizona and she couldn't bring herself to tell anyone why she was so depressed. For months, Edie pumped Claudia for information: *Is he dating anyone? Does he seem happy? You'd tell me if he mentioned me, right? Would Chad tell you?* Claudia was the only person she could be so utterly pathetic with. Her sister's disgust was aimed at Ridley, not Edie. What had Edie done wrong but fall in love with a charming man? How could she help it? After a little while, Edie got there, too. She'd made a mistake; she'd been young. Jesus, she was still young. And Claudia was even younger. It was stupid and irresponsible to get drunk and lose her phone, but hey, she hadn't gotten pregnant with a married man's baby! She didn't deserve Edie's snarky texts. Edie looked at Lydia and thought, *Claudia deserves to hold her niece.* "I hope she calls back soon."

But she didn't. Edie kept her phone next to her all that day and night, and nothing came in from her sister. When she called, Claudia's line went straight to voice mail. Edie scrolled to the app store and reinstalled Instagram, having to reset her forgotten password. Up rolled the lives. A guy she met at one of her dad's industry events five years ago posted an image of a coffee cup and a laptop. *#mindonmymoney*. A full-length mirror selfie by a woman who used to model with her mom. *#fashionmatters*. One of Claudia's friends lying on the deck of a boat. Blue sky, bikini, face tilted to the sun. *#yachtlife*. But nothing from Claudia since the night Edie went into labor.

The bra with the nipple-holes and the hospital-grade pump arrived. Nathan put the plastic pieces together and Edie fitted it all on her lumpy, wet-sand breasts. They flipped the switch and the sucking began, pulling milk that fell *drip drip drip* into the bottles attached.

"How does it feel?" asked Nathan.

She looked down. "It's kind of a relief. Like popping a zit."

Nathan laughed. "Gross." He was in a good mood. To him, giving birth in the city was an easy trade for the money to buy a house. He didn't have any drama with her parents and, although he would never say it, he probably thought it was pretty silly to pout about spending a month in a beautiful house where someone else cooked and cleaned and paid for everything. He didn't have anything to prove. And, of course, he was right. It was nothing. It was a made-up problem.

"When this is done," said Edie, "I want to go to the dorm. Claudia's phone is going to voice mail and she hasn't posted on social media in almost two weeks. I'm worried something's wrong."

"Like what?"

"I don't know. She's not texting my parents back, either. Maybe she's . . ." *What?*

"What?"

"I can get there and back in a cab. I'll be gone two hours, tops."

"I like your sister," said Nathan. "But this is a little crazy. She's making you come *find* her. You just had a baby."

"She's not making me. I need to get outside anyway. Everybody says that. I need some fresh air."

"I think it's a bad idea," said Nathan. He was choosing his words carefully. There was more he wanted to say. Something about hormones, probably. What had the doula called it? A hormone dump. Splat, it all comes out with the placenta. But Nathan wouldn't go there. He wasn't stupid.

"I'll be fine," Edie said.

EDIE

There were card-operated turnstiles to get into the dorm, so Edie had to approach the guard at the security desk. She'd never actually been in Claudia's suite. In fact, the only time Edie had been near campus since Claudia enrolled in NYU was to meet her sister for Christmas shopping at the Union Square market and then tea at the W hotel last year. Had Claudia asked her to go up and see where she lived? Edie didn't even remember.

"Excuse me," said Edie to a man in a gray uniform whose name tag read Stavros. "I'm going up to see my sister but I forgot what floor she's on."

"What's her name?" asked Stavros. Behind his desk was a short hall that appeared to lead to a labyrinth of post boxes and pantries. A girl emerged carrying a pack of toilet paper and a handful of mail.

"Claudia Castro."

"You're Claudia's sister?" asked the girl. Her hair was bleached white and her T-shirt read KEEP AUSTIN WEIRD. She set her load on the desk.

"Yeah," said Edie. "Do you know her?"

"I'm Rita," said the girl. "We're in the same suite, but I haven't seen her since break. Doesn't she stay at home a lot? That's what she told us."

"Sometimes," said Edie. "So, she hasn't been here?"

"We could be on different schedules. Maybe Whitney knows. They share a room. I'll take you up," she said. "I'm Rita."

Stavros buzzed Edie in. Rita picked up her toilet paper and mail and walked with her toward the elevator, pressed the button for the twelfth floor. "I should warn you, there's been some drama between Claudia and Whitney."

"I thought you hadn't seen Claudia?"

"I haven't, but Whitney's been talking. A lot."

"About what?"

The elevator doors opened and they stepped off. A girl talking on a phone tucked inside her hijab stood waiting to go down, a nylon bag of laundry at her feet.

"Long story short, Whitney had been hooking up with a guy, and then he started hooking up with Claudia. At least that's what Whitney says. I don't know all the details. I just know Whitney is super pissed."

Rita unlocked a door with four names on it: Whitney, Rita, Yuko, and Claudia. Whitney, Yuko, and Rita had each decorated their name tags with stickers (crosses and angels and a Dallas Cowboys star for Whitney; a Bernie sticker and comedy-tragedy mask for Rita; a magazine cut-out of Sarah Jessica Parker as Carrie Bradshaw for Yuko). Claudia, of course, couldn't be bothered. *Stickers? Really? Are we ten?*

Whitney, blond and bland, was in the suite, and just as Rita described, she was pissed.

"Claudia *knew* we were dating," she said. "Or, at least she *should* have known if she wasn't so self-involved. I mean, she's *seen* us together. I've *talked* about him."

"She's not here all the time, though," said Rita. "Like, almost never on weekends."

"She knew."

"So, when did all this happen?" Edie asked.

"They must have hooked up over spring break," said Whitney. "He brought her to church. It was insane."

"Church?"

"Oh, Trevor pretends to be a Christian. But he's a fucking *fake*. He's the fakest person I ever met."

"Okay," said Edie. She was annoyed at having to see through this girl's jealousy. Was what she said about this Trevor true? Or was she just jilted and angry? "When was the last time you saw her?"

Whitney shrugged. "I don't think she's been here since then."

"When?"

"Since she came to church last weekend. I haven't seen Trevor much, either. I figured they were off somewhere together."

"Can I look in her room?" asked Edie.

"Whatever." Whitney gestured toward the door behind her.

Edie wasn't sure what she was looking for, but there wasn't much of Claudia in the narrow room. Edie recognized a couple pairs of shoes and a Gucci bag that officially belonged to their mom. Whitney had photos pinned everywhere, but all that was on the wall beside Claudia's bed was a schedule for a yoga studio in Chelsea.

Whitney pointed Edie to Trevor's suite, and when she knocked, a young man wearing blue eyeliner answered the door.

"Don't tell me," he said, "you're looking for Trevor."

"I'm actually looking for my sister," said Edie. "Claudia Castro."

"Sorry," said the young man. "Didn't mean to be rude. My roommate is suddenly very popular. I'm Byrd. Claudia's not here. Neither is Trevor. Do you want to come in?"

They sat side by side on a futon covered in a scratchy wool blanket. The carpet desperately needed a vacuum.

"I haven't seen Trevor since Friday morning," said Byrd. Edie counted back. That was three days. "His laptop is gone and he didn't come to class today. He hasn't answered my texts, either."

"Did he say where he was going?" she asked.

"No. I assumed he was with Claudia. I guess she's MIA, too?"

"You guess?"

"The whole thing is kind of weird. I never actually saw

them together, but when I got back from break he was acting weird. And then he lost his phone. And then Whitney came over and had a little fit at him. She was like 'Claudia's a slut.' Sorry, that was her. So when she left I was, like, did you hook up with Claudia Castro? Because, I mean, that's a step up. He said no, but he was super cryptic. He was, like, something happened to her over break."

"Something happened? What does that mean?"

Byrd paused. "I'm sorry, that was a bad way of putting it. I really don't know. He was, like, she's all alone except for me. Which didn't make any sense. She's, like, kind of a celebrity, right? Anyway, I just figured it was drama. There's a lot of drama around here. But *then*, two different random guys came here looking for Trevor. One was older, in a suit. The other one said he was friends with Claudia."

"What did the friend look like?"

"He was our age. Really cute. Mixed-race, with sort of an afro."

Ben. She opened her phone, got on Instagram, and found a photo of Claudia's ex in her sister's feed. "Is this him?"

"Yeah, I think so."

Edie texted Ben immediately: *Is Claudia with you?*

Not even a minute later, Ben called back.

"Is she with you?" asked Edie.

"No," said Ben. "I've been trying to find her. Can you come over? There's something you need to see."

EDIE

Edie hadn't liked Ben Herman even before he started cheating on her little sister and calling it enlightened. Claudia had this idea that she'd won something when Ben asked her to be his girlfriend. *He's so talented*, she'd say. And yes, Ben had been well-reviewed for supporting parts in a couple off-Broadway shows, and did a three-episode arc on an HBO drama, but it wasn't like he'd just wandered into auditions and won everybody over: his father's production company won two Oscars and was bought by Disney before Ben was even born. It was sad, of course, that his dad had died, but when Edie looked at Ben she saw a person who'd never really had to work for anything. A good-looking guy with family money and lots of connections. She'd grown up with those guys; she'd been infatuated with her share. She knew all about them. Which is why she'd married Nathan.

They'd met walking across the Mid-Hudson Bridge early the spring before. Edie was finishing her senior year and not looking forward to going home, or to the Vineyard, for the summer. Claudia had just called with news that their parents had a big fight and their mom hadn't slept at the town house in almost a week. Edie went out for a walk and when she stopped to lean over the railing and look south toward the city, Nathan walked by.

"Gorgeous, right?" he said, smiling.

They hadn't been apart more than two days since, and when they were together they were at each other. Once or twice they ran out of condoms. When she told Nathan that she was pregnant, he asked what she wanted to do.

"I don't know yet," she said. "What do you want to do?"

"I know it's up to you, but if you want, I'm ready to just do this thing. Get married, start our lives. I can keep working for my family until I get something full-time."

They talked about all the options. Nathan's family owned a landscaping business and he made decent money planting gardens and mowing lawns and doing simple stone work. He'd gotten his degree in Environmental Science at Marist and was interviewing for jobs at some of the state parks in the area, hoping to eventually get into upper management. Edie was planning to apply to grad school and become a high school teacher, or maybe a guidance counselor. All through college she'd mentored girls in Poughkeepsie, helping them with their homework, taking them for ice cream, talking to them about contraception and consent. The irony. She could stay home with the baby for a year or two, then look for nearby or online programs that offered a master's in Education. They had Edie's trust fund money and they loved each other. What could go wrong? She was starting a new life! So, her patience for her sister's Ben Herman drama—which had always been thin—plummeted. It wasn't fair, she realized as she stood outside his brownstone. Claudia hadn't deserved her scorn.

Edie knocked, but when the big wooden door opened it wasn't Ben who appeared—it was Ridley Drake. Forty-whatever, dark suit, dark hair, brown eyes. Those eyes. She felt everything she'd felt that first night he'd put his hand on her leg at the club in Edgartown. His attention made her feel confident and beautiful. She'd been so stupid. She hadn't expected Ridley would propose when she told him she was pregnant, but she also hadn't expected that that would be the last conversation they'd have in person. Until now, five years later, when he was fucking her mom.

"Eden," said Ridley, putting his hand on her arm. He rubbed it lightly then leaned forward and kissed her cheek. "Congratulations. You look great."

He looked good, too. Like he always did. But something was different. He seemed edgy. That easy smile wasn't so easy.

"What are you doing here?" she asked.

He didn't answer. Ben appeared at the door.

"Don't let this change anything we just talked about," said Ridley.

"What?" asked Edie.

Ridley was already walking to the SUV idling at the curb.

"I was talking to Ben, honey," he said, not even turning

back. His driver stepped down from the front seat and opened the door.

"Have you seen Claudia?" she called.

Ridley didn't answer. He hopped up and into the car and was gone.

"Do you want to come in?" Ben asked.

"What's going on?" asked Edie, following him down the stone steps into the garden entry. They passed through the dark entry hall and into the living area. Edie had been here about two years before for Ben's graduation party. That night, the cavernous space was strung with lights and stuffed with people. Claudia had pointed to the interior balcony and giggled. *We had sex up there like two hours ago.* Empty and unlit, the room now felt like a mausoleum.

"Why was Ridley here?" she asked. "Have you seen Claudia?"

Ben stared at her, his eyes glazed. Was he stoned? "What do you want me to answer first?"

Before she could say, Edie's phone pinged. She pulled it from her pocket fast: *Please be Claudia.*

"Is that her?" asked Ben.

It was a text from Nathan: *are you ok? she needs to eat. should I give her a bottle of what you pumped?* Edie silenced the phone.

"No," she said. "When was the last time you saw her?"

"Last weekend."

"Why were you at her dorm?"

"What do you mean?"

"You're going to lie to me?" It was like talking to a child.

"I'm not lying, I'm just . . ." Ben gnashed his teeth and

groaned. The sound was low, like a moan, and it surprised Edie. Ben was in pain. "I don't know what to do. Last Sunday, the night after I saw Claudia, Chad Drake sent me a video. But he sent it to my old number and I didn't see it until a couple days ago."

"What's the video?"

Ben hesitated.

"Let me see it."

Ben handed over the phone, then turned away. Edie watched all fifty-eight seconds without breathing. Her sister's face, the bodies, the laughter. She began to shiver. Her heart itched in her chest, flaring like a rash. Chad Drake and some other guy raped Claudia. And filmed it.

"Why didn't you do something?" Edie said finally. Her voice was low and she spoke through her teeth, her tongue and lips weighted with what she'd seen.

"I did do something! I tried to find Claudia. I tried to find Chad." Ben dropped onto the sofa behind him. "*Why* would he send me a sex tape of him and Claudia?"

"Are you fucking kidding me, Ben? Does she even look *conscious* to you?"

"What?"

"You think that's a *sex tape*?"

"Stop yelling at me!"

Edie stopped. Ben was scared, too. Maybe he'd actually loved Claudia. She was never sure from the outside.

"Is that why Ridley was here?" she asked.

"I went to their building after I got this and the doormen

wouldn't let me up. Then, like an hour ago, Ridley showed up."

"Does he know where she is?"

"He said he doesn't."

"What about the video? Does he know about that?"

"I think so. He didn't say specifically, but he was, like, whatever happened between Claudia and Chad is their business. He was, like, as we both know, Claudia isn't exactly a virgin. And then he was, like, getting involved in this would be a mistake, son.'"

"He threatened you?"

"I mean, he didn't have a *gun*."

Actually, thought Edie, he might have. The summer they spent in bed together, Ridley showed her a handgun he'd just purchased. He was representing a football player who'd gotten caught picking up an underage girl in the Bronx, and the girl's pimp was bothering Ridley, asking for money to convince the girl not to testify. *It's not easy to get a gun permit in Manhattan*, Ridley had told her. He insisted she hold it and she remembered it had seemed enormous and frightening in her hands. Like it might spontaneously blast her in the face. She also remembered, with a cold shower of shame, that she'd found it sexy.

"When you saw her did she say anything about a guy she was dating? From school? Trevor?"

"She was with him at my party, but he didn't seem like her type."

"What do you mean?"

"He seemed intimidated by her."

Neither of them said anything for a few seconds. A horn blared outside. Another horn answered, louder and longer. Edie pulled out her phone.

"Who are you calling?" Ben asked.

"My mom."

EDIE

Ben gave her his phone, and on the way home Edie tried to turn what she'd learned in the last three hours into a path that led to her sister. But there was way too much she didn't know. When was the video made? And where? And what happened after it ended? Was Trevor involved? Who *was* Trevor? As the cab rolled past Union Square, Edie tried to ignore the growing anguish of her rapidly swelling breasts and started creating a story: Chad found out that Ridley was fucking their mom, and he decided it was his turn to bone a Castro girl. And Claudia, who'd felt bad for him since breaking his teenage heart, who saw Chad as pathetic when she should have realized he was dangerous, never saw it coming. Her sister was smart about so many things, but who could expect her to be smart about men yet? Edie remembered with a shudder that Claudia had texted her last fall after she'd drunkenly kissed Chad. Edie could have called—should have called. But she didn't. Instead, she'd sent a series of emojis: grimace, lol, facepalm.

The pressure in her breasts was almost unbearable when she finally got back to Gramercy. She walked in, breathless and bent over, her shirt now soaked with milk. Nathan was in the kitchen, and he wasn't happy.

"I just gave her a bottle," he said. "It's been almost four hours."

"I know. I'm sorry."

"Why didn't you answer my texts?"

"Can you get me the pump? And call my parents?"

"Edie, you can't just disappear."

"I didn't disappear! I was gone for a couple hours! You can't take care of her for a couple hours?"

"Whoa," said Nathan. "What's going on?

"Just . . . please." She looked around for the pump, gestured to her wet shirt. "Please. Can you help me with this?"

He did as she asked, and in ten minutes they were all gathered in the living room. Edie told her parents what she thought she knew and handed over Ben's phone.

"You don't have to watch the whole thing," she said. "But you have to watch a little so you understand."

After fifteen seconds, Gabe dropped the device. The sound continued. Chad's laugh. His disgusting voice. Nathan picked up the phone and silenced it. None of them spoke. The only sound in the room was the emphatic *squish squish* of the pump strapped to Edie's chest.

Edie's mom tucked her legs beneath her on the sofa. Her eyes looked like they'd moved closer together. It was as if what she'd seen had rearranged her features and they were now less symmetrical. Like the video was a mule that kicked her. "What did Ridley say to you at Ben's?"

"He barely said anything. I asked if he knew where she was and he ignored me. And Ben said that before I got there, he called Claudia a slut and told him not to get involved."

"Involved in what, exactly?" asked her dad.

"I don't know. But nobody's seen her at the dorm. Ben can't find her. And she's been hanging out with a new guy nobody really knows." Edie watched them take all this in. The next step was obvious, right? "I think we should call the police."

Her mother stood up and walked to the dining room table where her phone was. "I think we should call Jim first. His firm has a partner who handles things like this. She can give us advice."

"Why do we need advice?" asked Edie. "*That* happened to Claudia and now no one has seen her in a week. Something's wrong."

"And Jim will tell us what to do." Michelle started texting and pacing. "You don't want to get involved with the police, or Ridley, without a lawyer."

"Is that who you're texting? Ridley?"

"No, I'm not texting Ridley! What do you think I am?" Michelle's voice cracked. Edie had never seen her mother cry, and as she watched her struggle to compose herself Edie wondered, *who is the grown-up here? Who is going to take care of this?*

"I don't know if they can get here tonight, but probably first thing," said Michelle after a moment. "Jim's partner was in the Manhattan DA's office for years. Ingrid, that's her name. Her father was a state judge. She knows everybody."

"Can Jim get into Claudia's bank account?" asked Edie's dad.

"Yes," said her mom, a light coming into her eyes. "But so can we."

Gabe left the room, heading for the office computer on the garden level. Michelle's phone rang and she took it, hurrying upstairs. The pumps finished emptying Edie and she turned off the machine at her feet. Her hands shook as she unscrewed the half-full bottles. Careful not to spill. She set them on the coffee table, twisting a cap on each.

"I'm going to go talk to my dad," she told Nathan. Edie wrapped her sweater around her chest and closed her dad's office door behind her. She said it quickly: "The summer after high school I slept with Ridley and I got pregnant and he got me an abortion and I haven't talked to him since." And then: "Should I tell Mom?"

Her father sat silent at first, then he stood up and came over to her, wrapped his arms around her body, and let her cry.

"She probably thinks it's her fault Chad did that to Claudia," said Edie. "But I'm the one that brought them into our lives."

Gabe kept hold of her. "You aren't responsible for what Chad did. Neither is your mother. Let's focus on finding Claudia, okay? We need your mother strong right now." He lightened his embrace and looked at her, trying a smile.

"Thank you for telling me. You didn't do anything wrong. Do you understand that?"

She nodded, though she didn't agree. Maybe sleeping with Ridley wasn't wrong, but forgetting she had a sister the past two weeks was wrong. Chiding Claudia for being a party girl was wrong. She could have given her a break, but she hadn't. Edie wiped her eyes and sat on the office sofa.

"Did you find anything?" she asked.

"I was just about to log in to her account," said Gabe. He sat down and clicked at the computer.

"Oh my God," he said, leaning toward the screen.

"What?"

"Claudia withdrew fifty thousand dollars in cash last week."

Neither spoke for a moment.

"She could be anywhere," whispered Edie.

Jim Morgan and Ingrid Wythe arrived just after eight a.m. Jim, in his sixties, in a light gray suit, neck and face golf-tanned; Ingrid, her mom's age or a little older, tall and blond, toned by a trainer, dressed by a stylist. They all sat down in the living room and Jim explained that he had accessed Claudia's credit card and found almost two thousand dollars in charges at Macy's, another thousand at The Towers hotel in Times Square, and several hundred at a Bubba Gump restaurant.

"Bubba Gump in Times Square is literally the last place she would eat," said Edie.

"I've got a call in to the hotel," said Jim. "We need to

know if Claudia was the one using the card. The charges stop after the cash withdrawal. I'll call the bank as soon as we're done here. Ingrid has some other suggestions."

"Thanks Jim," said Ingrid. She leaned forward. Ingrid and Jim were the only people in the room wearing shoes. Nathan and Gabe hadn't left the house in days; even Michelle was disheveled. Her hair was clumped at the roots, shooting up at angles; her fluffy pink socks were gray with wear; she was getting a breakout of rosacea across her cheeks and upper lip.

"The hotel and the banks may have images of her on surveillance cameras," said Ingrid, "though some places don't keep the video more than a few days. We'll see. We want to know if she came in with anyone, or if someone else was using the cards in her name." She paused. "Jim told me about the video. I know this seems grotesque, but I'd like to see it."

Nathan found a pair of headphones and inserted them into the phone, then handed it to Ingrid. Her parents averted their eyes. Ingrid watched with an unchanged expression of concentration, then took off the headphones and handed the phone back to Nathan.

"Do you have any idea when this was recorded?"

"No," said Edie. "But the guy filming, the guy whose voice is loud, his name is Chad Drake."

Ingrid raised an eyebrow. "Jim mentioned a connection to Ridley Drake. We're sure this is his son?"

"Yes," said Edie.

Ingrid turned to Michelle. "I have to ask: When was the last time you spoke with Ridley?"

"Jesus," muttered Gabe.

Edie almost felt sorry for her mother. What had she told Jim? *And, I'm fucking the boy's father.*

"We texted yesterday morning," said Michelle. "Before I saw that."

"How close are you?"

Edie's mom sighed, then leaned forward into herself, her hand on her forehead. "We've been in the same circles forever. It's not love. Definitely not love."

Edie looked up at her mom, who was looking at her dad. Her dad was looking at the floor.

"And the last time you saw him?" Ingrid asked.

"It's been almost a week."

"Is that typical?"

"Typical?"

"Do you usually see each other more often?"

"It really depends on our schedules."

"He hasn't tried to contact you about this? Feel you out?"

"No."

"Okay, here's what I'm thinking," said Ingrid. "That video depicts a felony. Multiple felonies, actually. Sexual assault cases are absolutely the hardest cases to win in front of a jury. Worse than a murder without a body. But this video makes it a slam dunk."

"How?" asked Edie.

"You heard what he said about her peeing? It can be very difficult to prove a woman didn't consent to sex if she knows the man. Or men, in this case. Especially if she's been intimate with either of them before, or if she agreed to go home with even one of them. In most cases like this, where alcohol or drugs are involved, everything is circumstantial. Her past and her 'character' come into play. Basically, it's all going to be about her. She's both the victim and the accuser, so she's under a microscope. But even if she reported it the next day there's no way to test what was in her system when the sex happened. Maybe she was incapacitated or maybe she was just tipsy. There's a ton of reasonable doubt. Most prosecutors aren't eager to risk their conviction rate, and lots of women stop cooperating eventually. It's a nightmare.

"But." Ingrid paused dramatically. "The one almost surefire way to convince a jury that a woman was not capable of consenting to sex is if she loses control of her bodily functions. Plus, there's a new 'revenge porn' law aimed at people who pass around videos like this. With the right prosecutor, the asshole filming could easily spend twenty years in prison. Ridley Drake knows that."

Edie and her parents took this in.

"What are you telling us?" asked Gabe finally.

"What do you mean?" said Ingrid.

"Exactly what I said. What are you telling us? What should we do?"

"I'm not here to tell you what to do," said Ingrid.

"Well what the fuck are you here for?"

"I am here, Mr. Castro, because Jim told me that you are considering going to the police to report your daughter missing. If you do that, there are going to be a lot of questions and you need to be prepared for them. You say no one at her dorm has seen her in more than a week, she isn't answering her phone, and she hasn't been on social media. All that is concerning. But she also may or may not have checked into a hotel, and she may or may not have withdrawn a large sum of cash. Claudia is an adult. No one saw her being grabbed off the street. No one saw her get into a stranger's car. The only reason you have to believe she might be in danger is that video. And what I'm telling you is that that video is a can of worms. Half of the NYPD hates Ridley Drake, but the other half knows he pays extremely well for investigative assistance from former cops. They know he's got dirt on their bosses and their bosses' bosses, and they know that getting a DA to agree to bring a case against someone he's representing—let alone someone he's *related to*—is not going to be easy.

"Don't get me wrong, I am not saying you should do nothing. She might be in danger. Or she might come home when she's ready. There's no way to know. I'm just saying you need to be prepared." Ingrid paused again. "Take a few hours. You have my cell. I can meet you at the precinct if you want to go that way, or we can talk about hiring someone to do a bit of digging privately."

Jim and Ingrid showed themselves out.

"Was that supposed to make us feel better?" Edie asked. It occurred to her that without all the money, if it was Nathan's sister suddenly missing, they'd already be at the police station. Should they be?

The buzzer at the garden level door trilled through the walls.

"Did they forget something?" asked Michelle, looking around.

Gabe got up and went to the door.

"Hello?" Edie heard her father say.

A male voice, tinny over the speaker: "Hi. I'm a friend of Claudia's."

PART 3

CLAUDIA

Going back to the dorm where Jeremy and Chad lived was not an option. She ran across the street from where she'd vomited, leaving Daphne shocked and squealing, and raised her arm for a cab. "North," she said. In Times Square she saw the big hotel with the stupid restaurant on the ground floor and told the driver to stop. The lobby was scuffed marble and smudged mirrors and people in sneakers rolling oversized suitcases. She felt confident she would not encounter anyone she knew here. When it was her turn at the check-in desk, Claudia told the clerk with the eyebrow ring that she didn't have a reservation.

"How many nights?" the woman asked, typing.

Claudia had not thought of this. "Two. No. Three."

"I've got a junior suite on the fourteenth floor open for the next five nights."

"I'll take it."

The woman took her ID and her Visa and gave her an envelope with two key cards inside.

"Have a nice stay, Ms. Castro."

On the way to the elevator she saw an ATM and took out the maximum: $500.

The room faced west, overlooking the Hudson River and toward New Jersey. Her phone was off for now. She'd already missed the baby and she wasn't ready to handle the possibility that people would start messaging her about the video popping up somewhere. She looked at the bed and realized she didn't have anything to sleep in. She had the antibiotics and the PrEP pills in her purse, but not a toothbrush or a hairbrush or a change of clothes. Claudia took off her pants and the bra beneath her shirt, but when she climbed under the covers the sheets were cold and she felt exposed. Like something was going to creep up from the edge of the bed. She put her pants back on, filled up a glass with water, took her pills, and turned off the light.

In her dreams, her cell phone was too big. She couldn't slide it into her pocket. It kept growing, flashing, the video playing too loud. The laughing and the grunts and her silence bouncing off the walls of a bathroom stall. The water from the toilet running over. And she couldn't get the door open without putting down the phone. But the floor was filthy and now the room was lined with overflowing stalls going back into infinity.

She woke up the next morning and ordered pancakes that she didn't eat, then slept and stared at the television all day and all night. Twenty-four hours went by and she kept the blackout shades drawn. From the TV she learned that there had been another slashing. The fifth. So far people had been attacked on the R train, the 3 train, the sidewalk near the Astor Place station, the F train, and now a platform under the Barclays Center. The first victim was a teenage tourist from Missouri; the second a stay-at-home mom from Park Slope; the third a sophomore doing theater at Tisch. The teenager was leaving *The Lion King* with her parents, headed back to their Airbnb in Astoria. The mom was part of a group celebrating fortieth birthdays. The sophomore was apparently standing on the sidewalk smoking a cigarette and talking to her dad on the phone when the man appeared and ran a box cutter across her face. All but one of the victims were women and all the victims survived, but the news had all kinds of people talking about blood and screaming, and the police were still trying to get a decent description of the guy. Over and over Claudia read the word, heard the word: victim. *The victim's mother says her life will never be the same. The victim's husband says her children are afraid.* The victim the victim the victim. The word had spikes.

She turned off the TV but the suck of sudden silence, the loneliness, roared in her ears. She flipped it back on, lowered the volume, and lay down on the sofa, letting her eyes glaze and tear, letting herself cry. What happens next? She couldn't see anything past her headache; her hot, wet face; her mouth wide open on that video.

She slept through the afternoon again and awoke to see the red and orange lights of midtown glowing beneath the curtains. Claudia got off the couch and walked to the window. She looked down at the mirrored glass and the glare off the river: it was beautiful. She was ugly now; sick, infected—but the world was still full of beauty. And that made her mad.

The bar at Bubba Gump's was crowded but there was an open stool at the end, and she slid in between the tray of garnishes and a blonde. Claudia knew she looked young but she also knew her ID was good. She asked for a vodka and soda and a menu. The blonde smiled at her.

"Can I ask you somethin'?"

"Sure," said Claudia.

"It one hundred percent counts as catfishin' if you fake the profile photo *and* the age, right?"

"Yeah, I think so."

"See!" she shouted at the bartender, whose name tag read Frankie. Frankie put up his hands in mock surrender.

"Girl, we been through this before."

"I don't know the rules anymore!" The blonde turned to Claudia. "I just got out of a relationship."

"Your boyfriend dumped your ass at *Halloween*, Lesley," said Frankie. "It's been a while."

"Can I help I'm too trusting?"

"I don't trust anybody anymore," said Claudia.

"Oh, shit," said Frankie. "You too young to be like that."

Lesley put her arm around Claudia.

"She's *smart*," said Lesley. "I wish I was a little smarter sometimes."

Frankie set the vodka and soda in front of Claudia. "You said it, I didn't."

Lesley laughed. "Cheers to smart bitches."

Cheers. Lesley began to talk. She was from "outside Atlanta," worked at Hooters ("I transferred up . . . It's actually a great company!") and lived in Bay Ridge. She'd moved to New York for a guy she met online two years before. He worked "in finance" and lived in Murray Hill in a "nice" one-bedroom "with a doorman."

"My mom was happy about the doorman," she said. "She was certain I was gonna get raped when I moved here. I was, like, *Mom*, New York is the safest big city in the country! You know that, right? It's crazy, but it's true. I looked it up. Anyway, he literally broke up with me *on* Halloween. While I was wearin' my costume."

"Tell him what you were," said Frankie.

"I was a sexy bride."

Frankie howled a laugh shook. "I felt sorry for her. I did."

"And it's been love ever since," said Lesley, blowing him a kiss.

Frankie rolled his eyes. "I said I *did*. I don't have no sympathy for bitches who don't learn."

Lesley told Claudia that she came here to meet her online dates because it was near her job and reminded her of home. Apparently she had a lot of online dates.

"I gotta find somebody to pay the rent!" She laughed and Frankie, who was refilling the maraschino cherries, slapped her a high-five. As if on cue, the two exclaimed: "The rent is too damn high!"

Claudia ordered dinner for them both and another round of drinks. Lesley was drinking Chardonnay, so Claudia switched to that. Men came up to the bar and tried to talk to them, but Lesley shooed them away.

"We're having a *girls'* night," she said, and turned her back.

At midnight, Lesley announced that she had to get home.

"No sleep till Brooklyn," she said. "That's how you say it, right, Frankie?"

"Yeah, but it's never gonna sound right coming outta your mouth."

Claudia signed the bill and, as casually as she could possibly manage, turned to Lesley and said, "Crash in my room. I've got a suite."

Lesley, Claudia had learned at the bar, had two online personas: one for friends and family back home, and one she used for dating. Friends and family Lesley Swaine was the thirty-one-year-old Lesley smiling in her orange Hooters shorts, drinking beer on a blanket in Central Park, posing with the bull's balls on Wall Street. Dating Leslee Lincoln was twenty-eight, wore black dresses and crossed her legs and drank champagne. Leslee Lincoln listed her occupation as "concierge, Southern Belle," and Leslee Lincoln agreed to swipe right on Chad's profile when they got up to the room. Less than five minutes later he responded.

hey Belle—lost in the big city?

"Can I write him back?" asked Claudia.

"Sure," said Lesley, handing her the phone. "Is there anything in the fridge?"

"Take whatever you want," said Claudia. "We can call room service, too."

Lesley chose a mini white wine. She unscrewed the top and drained half the bottle in a single swallow.

Claudia typed: *hopelessly!*

Lesley offered the bottle to Claudia for a sip and Claudia took it. Why not? She almost felt like smiling. This was going to be so easy.

"So, what's the plan?" asked Lesley. "Who is this guy?"

"We used to be friends and he got the wrong idea."

Lesley drank more wine and nodded her head. Claudia felt understood so she told Lesley her idea; well, most of it. The part she needed to know.

"I know a guy who has ketamine," Lesley said.

It was perfect. Claudia made her offer: "I'll give you five thousand dollars if you get him to meet you at the bar, put some in his drink, and bring him up here."

Lesley closed one eye and squinted at Claudia, assessing. She was drunk, but it occurred to Claudia that Lesley might be the kind of person who performed much of her life while drunk. Her mom's cousin Allison was like that; wine with lunch and then never without a drink in her hand until bedtime. Years ago, on the Vineyard, she and Edie saw Allison throwing up in the bushes. They told their mother Cousin Allison was sick. *She's not sick*, said Michelle. *She's drunk. Ali's usually drunk. In five years she'll be twenty years older.* Her mom had been right. At barely forty-five, Allison's face and legs were swollen. Last summer she fell in the house and sliced her arm on the broken wineglass she'd been holding. Claudia remembered

Allison's scream and the blood smeared on the floor. Nathan was the only one who had any idea what to do.

"Five *thousand* dollars," said Lesley.

"Plus whatever the ketamine costs."

"What's the time line?"

"Soon as possible. I'll give you half tomorrow. I'll go to the bank first thing."

"What happens after I get him up here?"

"You leave."

"Then what happens?"

"I give you the rest of the money."

Lesley lifted the mini wine bottle.

"I'm in, girl. Cheers."

TREVOR

Trevor sent her a dozen texts, but three days after he brought her to church, Claudia had dropped out of contact. It hurt, but he got it. She was embarrassed and traumatized and she needed time alone. On Wednesday, Whitney knocked to see if he was coming to Bible study.

"Is Claudia here?" she asked, peeking her head into the suite.

"No."

"Don't get *mad*. So, you're hooking up with her now?" She pushed past him. "You owe me the truth. Don't you think?"

"I don't owe you anything."

Whitney hadn't expected that. She grabbed his phone.

"Let me just check . . . Oh! There she is. Claudia! Claudia! Where are you?"

She was walking backward, scrolling, her beady little eyes grabbing as much information as they could. Trevor reached for the phone but she was prepared, twisted back. He wanted to push her, hard, right out the door. He felt it in his stomach and his hands. He wanted her to fall. He wanted her to hurt. He wanted her to hurt for being whole while Claudia was shattered. She was going to make a scene about a freshman hookup? Privileged bitch. She'd never known anything but easy her whole life. He grabbed her wrist and she dropped the phone.

"I hate you," she said.

"Whitney, you don't know what you're talking about. I'm sorry things didn't work out between us. I really am."

She was crying before she got out the door. He picked up the phone. Each time he checked his texts and Claudia hadn't written back, Trevor hated Chad Drake more. Sending that video was an act of aggression. Chad might as well have punched him in the face and laughed. Was he supposed to just take it? Turn the other cheek?

Trevor got up early the next morning, put on a pair of sunglasses, and stood outside their dorm on Fourteenth Street. He didn't have to wait long: At nine forty-five Chad walked out of the building and Trevor trailed him down University and into the library. He waited across the street, on a bench outside the park, and two hours later Chad came out and hailed a cab. Trevor did the same, saying, just like in the movies, "Follow that taxi." Trevor held on to the strap above the window and leaned forward, watching FT778 jerk and speed uptown. The driver was listening to talk radio.

"Can you turn that down?" Trevor asked.

"What?"

"It's hard to think."

The driver lowered the volume.

Chad got out uptown, in front of a fancy building on Fifth Avenue. Trevor gave the driver too much cash and jumped out.

"Chad!"

Chad stopped. Trevor hadn't settled on what he was going to say when he caught up with him, and when Chad saw him hesitate, he laughed.

"Why did you send me that video?" asked Trevor.

"What video? I didn't send any video." Chad's grin was egregious.

"I know it was you. Claudia knows it was you."

"Whatever. Claudia Castro's a fucking liar."

"You're a rapist."

"Oh, please."

"She was drunk."

"She didn't say no."

Trevor hit him, fist to face, and Chad stumbled back, fell onto the green carpet beneath the green awning that announced The Park View. Two doormen in green coats and hats came running. The tall one grabbed Trevor by the arms while the other knelt next to Chad, who jumped up, ran toward Trevor, and punched him in the stomach. Trevor's knees buckled and the tall doorman let go. Chad stepped back and kicked him in the face. Trevor tasted blood and kept his head down. He'd made a mistake coming here. He wasn't helping anybody. He needed to get home.

"If Claudia Castro doesn't want people to know she's a slut, she should stop being one," said Chad. The balding doorman tried to take Chad's arm but he shook him off. "I'm fine."

Trevor was still on hands and knees on the green carpet. Maybe he'd sink into the sidewalk.

"Call the police," said Chad. "I want to press charges."

"Mr. Drake," began the balding doorman.

"What did I just say? Call. The. Police."

"Your father . . ."

"My father what? Oh Jesus fucking Christ, I'll do it." Chad rubbed his jaw and pulled his phone from his back pocket.

Trevor stood up. Breathing hurt. Where was he? People were starting to gather around the green carpet: two women in yoga pants; another talking into her earbuds, pushing a double stroller. He was a long way from his dorm. Was there a subway nearby? He looked to the street. A taxi. All he needed to do was raise his arm. He started to walk, but Chad began shouting and the tall doorman grabbed his wrist.

"I've gotta go," Trevor said.

The doorman did not release his grip. His green cap had fallen off.

Should he run? The crowd seemed to have tripled in size, and then there was a police officer. Trevor let himself be walked into the building and down an ornately carved, wood-paneled hallway, his sneakers soft on the oriental rugs that lined the floor like dominos laid end-to-end. He sat where the wide-chested cop told him to sit, in a little room that appeared to be a sorting facility for packages.

After a minute, a second officer, a woman who couldn't have been older than twenty-five, arrived, and Chad started talking.

"He followed me home and attacked me."

The officers listened and made notes and asked the doormen to describe what they'd seen.

If they arrested him, who would he call? Should he tell them why he was there? Should he defend himself? But he didn't have to do either, because while Chad was detailing how he'd been stalked and ambushed, a man in a dark suit walked in.

"Stop talking, Chad," said the man.

"Dad, he followed me—"

"What did I just say?"

Chad stopped talking.

"Mr. Drake," said the balding doorman, "we left a message with your office . . ."

"Not now, Martin," said Chad's father, taking a business card from a pocket inside his jacket. "Officers, my name is Ridley Drake. I am an attorney. This is my son and I'd like to speak with him alone for a moment if you don't mind."

The officers looked at each other. The man, Officer Sanchez by his name tag, appeared to make the decision for them both.

"Come with us, son," said Sanchez. He motioned for Trevor to follow.

Was this it?

"I'll be just a moment," said Mr. Drake. "I do appreciate the courtesy."

Back in the entry hall, Trevor stood in a circle with the cops and the doormen. The tall one took off his hat and scratched his head.

"That was exciting," he said.

"The last time I was in this building was when Mrs. Wisner's grandson OD'd," said Officer Sanchez.

"So, why'd you hit him?" asked the female cop, Officer Malone. Her hair was pulled back into a short ponytail and she wore a bulletproof vest under her shirt.

Claudia had not given him permission to talk about what Chad and Jeremy had done. And she certainly hadn't given permission to tell the police about it. He wanted to say it so badly: *Because he raped my friend and took a video of it.* But he didn't.

"Because he's a dick," Trevor said.

The tall doorman laughed and the door to the storage room opened. Mr. Drake stepped out with Chad behind him, looking deflated.

"My son has decided against pressing charges," he said. "We're willing to call it a schoolyard fight, slightly off campus. How does that sound, son?"

"Fine," said Trevor. "Can I go now?"

TREVOR

The big black car was waiting for him the next morning, as if his night spent obsessing had conjured the man up. Dark hair, dark suit, dark sunglasses, standing beside an open door.

"Trevor," said Ridley Drake. "Do you have a minute?"

Trevor slid over on the dark leather seat and Ridley sat down beside him, pulling the door closed. The driver, also wearing a dark suit and sunglasses, checked his mirror and pulled into the traffic on Fourteenth Street.

"Where are we going?" asked Trevor.

"We'll just drive a bit. I can drop you wherever you'd like. Do you want something to drink?" Ridley opened a console in the center of the vehicle that held water and flavored seltzer and glass bottles of beer.

"I'm okay."

Behind them, in the third row, sat a younger man with a

thin face and close-set eyes. Instead of a suit, he wore a polo shirt and he was typing on a laptop balanced on his knees.

"This is Eric, one of my associates," said Ridley.

Eric nodded but continued typing.

Ridley took off his sunglasses. "I'm sorry to sneak up on you. First of all, I want to apologize for what happened yesterday. There was absolutely no reason to involve the police, for Christsakes. Total overreaction. I'm going to be straight with you: My son is a fucking idiot. He has had literally every advantage. He's good-looking, he's athletic, he's intelligent. But he's a fucking idiot. Especially when it comes to girls, and especially when it comes to Claudia Castro. He's been with other girls. I know that for certain. But he wants the one he can't have. And she knows exactly what she's doing, stringing him along. And this has been going on for years, okay? Have you met her family? Mom, sister?"

Trevor shook his head.

"Well, let's just say she comes by it honestly."

Ridley paused. For effect? Behind him, Eric's clicking continued. The car stopped for a yellow light. What street were they on?

"After you left yesterday, Chad and I had a talk. I'm very, very sorry he sent you that video. Like I said, he's an idiot. And impulsive, which is at least as bad. What kind of work does your father do?"

"What?"

"Your father. What's his job?" Trevor hesitated. Ridley didn't care about his father, and Trevor suspected that if he didn't say anything, the man would just keep talking. He was right. "I'm an attorney. And I don't hide my work from my son. The fact that he would record himself having sex and then pass it around . . . I mean, it's just insane. But that's what Claudia Castro does to him. Have you shown the video to anyone else?"

"No." Trevor straightened his shoulders. Did he just blame Claudia for what Chad had done?

"Right, why would you? Again, I'm sorry you had to see that. And like I said, I understand why you did what you did yesterday. If someone had shown me that of my girlfriend . . ."

"She's not my girlfriend."

"Okay, well, your *whatever*. I'm saying I don't blame you. Chad will pay for this, I assure you. There will be consequences at home. Strings will be tightened significantly. But I don't believe—and I hope you don't believe—that one mistake should ruin a boy's life."

Trevor almost laughed. Chad was older than his brother had been when he went to prison. Eighteen was old enough for Michael Barber to have his life ruined. But not Chad Drake? And all his brother had done was sell weed, and sometimes a little Molly or mushrooms, to friends; Chad Drake was a rapist. But Chad Drake had Daddy Ridley. Trevor's father had to start driving an Uber to pay for the lawyer after both his boys were arrested that icy Sunday afternoon at the duplex on Maple. Trevor had never tagged along with his big brother to the house where he got his supply before, but they'd gotten high together that morning and Mike promised

Dunkin' on the way. Trevor stayed in the car with the donuts while his brother ran in. Mike was a senior with a B-average; the definition of small time. The goofy, long-haired kid who carried the party with him, earning just enough for some pocket money, a payment on the Camry, and a chunk into the college fund. He went to Maple barely once a month for a backpack full of product. But he was there, they were both there, when the cops raided the place and found way more than weed.

Trevor might have avoided being arrested if he'd just stayed in the car, but when the cruisers pulled up he panicked and ran. The neighborhood was unfamiliar, and as he heard the boots behind him getting closer, he looked back and tripped. So they handcuffed him, threw him in the waiting van, drove him rough downtown, and made him spend the night. Mike was booked into the jail and stayed for almost a week, until Trevor's dad could get into his 401(k) for the bail. The retainer for taking both boys' cases was $10,000 and a month later the lawyer suggested they make a deal: community service for Trevor, a juvenile; eighteen months behind bars for Mike. And a felony on his record forever.

In his letters, Mike wrote to Trevor about keeping his chin up. *Get back to church*, he'd advise. *Ignore the bullshit. Give yourself a second chance.* So Trevor stood in the pews with his parents every Sunday at Grace Christian Fellowship. He went to Wednesday evening Bible Study and he went on spring break mission trips and he was a summer counselor at a Baptist camp in Pennsylvania. Sometimes he let himself feel that love Jesus supposedly wanted to give him. He prayed for strength and he thought about justice. Mike loved hearing the stories of the girls who wanted to stay technical virgins. *I bet you do just fine*, he wrote back. And it was true. Mike's letters came weekly, long missives where his big brother considered where he'd gone wrong and imagined a better path for himself. But the path was never going to be better. The path was no student loans for felons. No Section 8 for felons. Limited professional licensing for felons. Even more limited jobs. The path, when he got out in the middle of Trevor's senior year, was living at home, scrounging for work from friends' parents, online classes, depression, weed. Trevor tiptoed around his brother's molten anger and his parents' increasing desperation; he kept his grades up and his head down, and when the thick packet from NYU came in the mail the next spring, his mother and father took him out for lunch and told him they were thrilled and proud but that they didn't want to make too big a deal at home.

"Your brother is happy for you, too," said his dad. "We just need to be mindful of how he's feeling right now."

Trevor almost wept, right there over his steaming fajitas. He'd spent his whole life looking up to his brother. His funny, creative, kind, capable brother. Mike was a grown man, and here they were, the people who knew him best, talking about him like he was a fucking baby.

So should one mistake ruin poor Chad's life? Yes.

That's exactly what it should do. But he wasn't going to argue the point with Ridley Drake. Ridley Drake was summa cum laude at arguing. The night before Trevor had been thinking about what the lawyer in Canton told them about the deal that took his brother's life away from him: *It's the best I can get.* The DA wants to make a point, said the lawyer. Selling drugs to teenagers will not be tolerated in Canton. Selling drugs to teenagers will ruin your life. The lawyer said the DA wouldn't listen to reason but Trevor suspected something different. Trevor suspected the DA wouldn't listen to their lawyer. Because $10,000 wasn't enough for a lawyer people listened to. It wasn't enough for a lawyer like what Chad got for free.

"Sure," said Trevor.

"I'm glad you agree," said Ridley. "And let's be honest, I can't imagine Claudia wants to extend this situation any further."

Trevor nodded.

"Have you made any copies of the video? Uploaded it anywhere?"

"No."

"That's what I was hoping." Ridley brought a briefcase onto his lap and snapped it open. "We agree that nobody wants this video to go any farther than it's already gone. I've destroyed Chad's phone and computer. What I'd like to do is make an exchange with you. This is a brand new iPhone. The latest model. Uri is going to pull up to a cell phone store where we can set it up with your number and the bill will go to me for the next year. "

Chad's father then pulled a yellow envelope from the briefcase.

"I realize there is some inconvenience involved and I want to offset that." He paused. "This is ten thousand dollars."

Trevor stared at the envelope. Saliva gathered in his mouth.

"What about Claudia?" asked Trevor.

"She's very emotional right now. No girl wants to look like a slut. And definitely not so . . . graphically."

"You talked to her?"

"She doesn't want this to get out, either."

Eric *click-click*ed in the back seat and Uri made a right turn.

"The cell phone store is just up here," said Ridley. "We'll pop in and then take you wherever you need to go."

"I think I'm going to keep my phone," said Trevor.

"Oh, come on now. This is found money, son. You just won the lottery."

"Could you pull over?"

"Don't be stupid, Trevor. What are you going to do? Jerk off to it?"

"I want to get out."

"I can give you twenty thousand dollars right now. Cash."

Uri stopped at a red light and Trevor opened the door. Horns honked as he stumbled onto whatever street he was on.

He hopped the curb to the sidewalk and started walking fast. At the corner he looked up: Thirty-Ninth Street. There was a subway at Forty-Second Street—he knew that. He kept walking. When he got to Forty-Second Street, he asked a hot dog vendor which way to the subway. The vendor pointed. His phone rang as he was crossing Park Avenue. It was Claudia.

Trevor stopped walking. The woman behind him ran into his ankles with a stroller.

"Asshole!" she shouted.

He stepped out of the middle of the sidewalk and beneath the awning of a plus-sized ladies clothing store. A homeless man was slumped there, dressed in oily winter clothing, his boots half off, ankles swollen hard red and purple.

"Claudia?"

"Can you hear me?"

"Yeah."

"I'm sorry I haven't texted you back. I turned my phone off. I haven't talked to anybody."

"It's okay." The relief he felt at the sound of her voice was breathtaking. He couldn't help how much he wanted her. He wanted her more than he wanted twenty thousand dollars. They were going to get through this together. "Did you talk to Ridley?"

"Who?" asked Claudia.

"Chad's dad."

"What are you talking about? Where are you?"

"Forty-Second Street."

"I'm in a hotel on Forty-Fourth. The Towers in Times Square. There's a Bubba Gump on the corner. Room 1492."

Sailed the ocean blue, he thought as he began walking. He had only gone half a block when the man ran into him, snatched his phone, pushed him toward the street, and disappeared into the crowd.

CLAUDIA

"What should we do?" asked Trevor after he'd told her about his encounters with Chad and Ridley.

"We?"

"Those assholes came after me, too."

Claudia was ready with her answer: "I have to assume that video is going to get out. When it does, the story isn't going to be: Claudia Castro is a slut. The story is going to be: The guys who fucked with Claudia Castro got fucked up."

"I want to help you."

They decided that step one was to get Claudia out of the hotel, where she was registered under her name. Whatever was going to happen next had to happen with a minimal footprint. She'd turned on her phone on that morning and deleted all the social apps. Texts were mostly from Trevor and her mom. Mom requesting a "family meeting"; Mom saying Edie "needs her sister." They were easy to ignore. But after what had happened to Trevor's phone, Claudia realized that having hers on made her vulnerable to GPS tracking. Ridley had his lawyer fingers in with all kinds of hackers. Chad once told her that was how his dad got a better deal in the divorce: He got into Chad's mom's phone and got proof she'd been having an affair, too. *She paid up rather than look like a slut,* Chad said. How could she have ever thought they were friends? The whole time, he just wanted to shove himself into her. To make her his.

She and Trevor went downstairs to the hotel's business office to use the Internet. A few clicks and they found an open room at a Holiday Inn on Ninth Avenue. Her fake ID said she was Ingrid Greggs twenty-two, of Yonkers, and she figured that with enough cash up front, she could convince the desk clerk to overlook a "lost" credit card.

Step two was the bank.

"I'm gonna run some errands," she told Trevor. "Meet me at the hotel in an hour?"

He didn't make her explain further.

She walked into a Bank of America branch on Forty-Second Street, but the ATM had a $2,000 daily withdrawal limit. That wasn't going to cut it. She needed $5,000 for Lesley. Plus who knew how many nights in the hotel after this. And maybe a plane ticket? And she should give Trevor something to make up for what he lost when he told Ridley to fuck off. Claudia knew she had nearly $70,000 in her personal checking. Jim Morgan transferred $5,000 from the family's account into hers every month, and since coming to college she'd cut back on clothes and shoes and bags. It was one of her resolutions when she started at NYU: less stuff, more experiences. Aerial yoga and live music and even tasting menus were cheaper than designer dresses, so the money piled up. To get as much out as she wanted, though, she was going to have to show her real ID. Hopefully it would be worth it. From behind the glass doors leading into the branch Claudia assessed the tellers for the one she thought would ask the fewest questions. She picked well and when she told "LUIS"—clean-cut but young enough not to be suspicious of light flirting from a teenager—that she wanted to withdraw fifty thousand dollars cash because she was going to Vegas, all he asked was, "Can I come, too?"

She and Trevor both needed new phones, so the next stop was the T-Mobile store, and then Macy's, for something to wear; jeans and T-shirts, a jacket, a week's worth of underwear, and a pair of boots she could walk in. Downstairs at the Louis Vuitton counter she bought a duffle bag to carry it all.

At the Holiday Inn, they ordered a pizza to the room and Claudia told Trevor what she had planned with Lesley. He was, she imagined, a little bit impressed. Or maybe she wasn't reading him right.

"What about the other one?" he asked. "Jeremy."

"Do you know him?"

"No. But I saw him in the hall the other day. He was knocking on your door."

"Was he carrying his guitar?"

"I think he always is."

"Exactly," said Claudia. "Check this out."

She pulled up Google on the new phone, searched "Jeremy Cahill," and clicked the first link, a local news article from a couple of weeks before:

NYU BAND WINS GREEN DAY CONTEST

By Lina Malloy

An NYU freshman and his band are the winners of a national search for the next great rock stars sponsored by Green Day.

"This is such an amazing opportunity to get our music to a wider audience," said lead singer and guitarist, Jeremy Cahill, 19.

Cahill is a Music major and says he and his bandmates in "Rock" just started playing together last fall.

"We were on the same vibe from the first day of practice."

In a statement on their website, Green Day's front man, Billie Joe Armstrong, said that "Rock" was "the most original, exciting band we heard . . . we can't wait to get them in the studio."

Rock's other members are Chris Azarian, 19; Dante Nilsson, 21; and Kingston Wilcox, 22.

"What a douche," said Trevor. "*It's such an amazing opportunity to share our music.* Does anybody even listen to Green Day? They're, like, fifty."

Claudia laughed. "Any ideas?"

Trevor thought about it. "What if he couldn't play the guitar anymore?"

JEREMY

It was raining Friday when Jeremy Cahill's father called and asked if he'd take a late LIRR train home so he could get up early and help with the front gutter, which had come loose again.

"Your brother is working double shifts or I wouldn't ask," his father said when they spoke. "When your record drops you can hire me a groundskeeper!"

Peter Cahill mentioned the Green Day contest in one way or another every time they spoke, and Jeremy had stopped reminding his father that he had not won an entire album contract, but a contract to record a single. Or at least that was his understanding. It had been a month since they got the news, and details were still scarce. There had been a meeting around a conference table at the record label in Midtown, and a tour of a recording studio, though not, apparently, the studio they were going to record their song in. The executive said it would all be worked out later.

Rock was only five months old when they entered the contest with the song Jeremy had written and that they'd set down in an NYU studio. Four guys: Kingston Wilcox, the drummer who'd dropped out of Juilliard and who Jeremy met at a gig in Brooklyn; Chris Azarian, a freshman from California, who played bass and sang backup; Dante Nilsson, an enormous Wisconsin-bred farm boy who'd taught himself a dozen instruments by the time he was twelve, and played keyboards, trumpet, harmonica, and, in a pinch, rhythm guitar; and Jeremy Cahill, lead guitar, lead vocals. They called the band Rock because their mission was to rock. Let Sam Smith and Nick Jonas get you laid, Rock was going to get you on your feet. Get you moving. Rock played get-drunk-and-dance music. Everybody loved it. They could have played two gigs every night, but Jeremy was choosey. Right after they announced the contest winners, City Winery called and said Steve Earle wanted them to open for him at his monthly show. Jeremy turned them down.

"It's all tables and chairs and people sitting there eating," he said to the guys. "It won't work."

"But it's Steve Earle," said Dante. "He can hook us up with a lot of people."

"Not if we play a shit show. I'm telling you, you're gonna get up on that little stage and look out at all those moms and dads eating their fucking crostini and sipping wine and you're gonna lose your hard-on. Trust me. We gotta play where we can really *play*. Steve Earle is, like, seventy. He's cool but he's cruising. That's not us. We gotta stick with the brand. Rock doesn't do dinner theater."

The record company had tied the announcement of the winners of the "Green Day on Campus" contest to the band's world tour and Jeremy and all the guys from Rock got floor seats and backstage passes to the show at Madison Square Garden. In the green room, the band stood around waiting for Billie Joe, who they had been assured wanted to meet them. When he finally appeared, shorter than them all, with wild black hair and eyeliner and high-top sneakers, he was in a hurry to get on stage, but took a minute to shake everybody's hand and congratulate them.

"Really fantastic playing," Billie Joe said to Jeremy when he introduced himself as lead guitarist. "Great song, but I'll tell you what put me over for you guys was that guitar intro. You write that?"

"Yeah," said Jeremy. He'd written the whole song.

"Man, I wish I'd come up with that! I couldn't stop thinking about it. That fingering isn't easy. I've been playing guitar all day every day for thirty-five years and it took me a minute to get it. But it feels like I should know it already, you know? Like it's gonna be part of the *canon*. Dire Straits. The Who. The Kinks. You guys are, what again?"

"We're Rock," said Jeremy.

"Rock. Okay, okay, I dig it. Rock. Fuck yeah. Rock."

A stagehand brought them back into the audience just as the lights went down in the arena. Everybody was ready to rock. Thousands of people squirming and shouting and whistling in anticipation of getting to experience three men playing their music. Jeremy looked around him and felt certain that this was his future. How could it not be?

About halfway through their set, Billie Joe came to the microphone:

"We've got a seriously talented guitarist in the audience tonight, everybody. He and his band just won our 'Green Day on Campus' contest and you all are gonna hear that single soon. I promise, I promise, you'll love it. So, Jeremy? You down there, mate? Not in the loo?" Billie Joe put his hand over his face to shade his eyes from all the stage lights. "There you are! Come on up. Think you can handle 'American Idiot'?"

Jeremy didn't even look at his boys; he took the metal stairs to the stage two-by-two. He had willed it into happening. Someone handed him a guitar and he strummed a few chords and they were off.

"Dude, this is officially the best night of your life so far, right?" said Dante when the concert was over and they were riding the escalator down to the subway below Penn Station.

"A hundred percent," said Jeremy.

"Where should we go?"

"Somewhere cheap," said Chris. "And not exclusively hetero."

"On the best night of my life so far I want to get laid," said Jeremy. "I want to fuck a hot chick."

"You can do it, man!" said Dante. He swept his arm around at the teeming masses of sweating Green Day fans above and below them. "The city is your oyster. Ladies! Ladies! Do you recognize this man? He played tonight!"

Scattered laughs and a couple shouts of "Woo-hoo!" emboldened him.

"He's single!"

"So's she!" A brunette half a floor below them waved her arm and pointed at her friend, a blonde. The brunette was wearing a T-shirt with the word "*Bride*" on it in glittery letters. The blonde and the half dozen women around her were wearing matching pink "*Bridesmaid*" T-shirts. The blonde had her face in her hands for a moment, then pushed her friend and laughed.

"It's true!" she shouted.

"Jeremy?" said Dante. "What do you think? Swipe right?"

"Get her number!" shouted the bride. The bridesmaids shrieked and applauded. People started taking out their phones. *Get her number! Get her number!*

Jeremy stopped at the landing, his friends jumping up and down behind him, and greeted the blonde. She was older than him. Thirty? Maybe thirty-five. She wasn't awful but she was not the hot chick he was going to fuck tonight. He and the boys were not following a bachelorette party to some dumb club—though Chris might have loved that.

"I'm Beth," she said. She was smiling but she looked sad. Jeremy figured maybe she'd just been dumped. "Sorry, my friend is drunk and crazy. You were great up there."

"Thanks. Wanna give me your number?"

He put it into his phone under "Beth"—no real point in

asking a last name. She was probably from Long Island just like him. Probably worked in a health club or a bank. She couldn't get him anywhere.

"Thanks, Beth," he said, winking. It all felt like a performance. "I'll text you."

And then he kissed her. Grabbed her around the waist and laid one on her. The crowd went wild. Beth didn't push him off and when he pulled away she was laughing. She waved and pushed up the escalator back to her cheering friends in pink and white. Jeremy took a bow.

The plan was to get a drink and a shot at the Bryant Park restaurant where Jeremy's brother, Lars, tended bar, then head back to the Village. Lars had been working for the same restaurant group for more than a decade, first in Rockville Center in high school, then the Upper East Side, now Midtown. Lars would hook them up for a couple rounds, and after that they'd go to Down Under on Bleecker, where their IDs worked. Down Under had three-dollar PBRs, and Chris had once gotten a blow job in the bathroom from a stage manager at the Lucille Lortel.

Bryant Park was crowded. Green Day fans loading up before heading down into Grand Central and the train home to wherever; workaday men and women in bad suits, held too late at the office; and tourists on expense accounts, red-faced and handsy, sleeves rolled up, signaling the waitstaff for more more more.

"How was it?" shouted Lars from behind the bar, waving them over. Dante and Kingston and Chris talked over themselves to tell of his little brother's triumphs. Shots were poured and pounded.

"This kid got our mother's talent and her looks," said Lars.

"What'd you get, Lars?" asked a man who looked like a regular. Shaggy gray hair, yellowing moustache, a Levon Helm T-shirt.

"I got you bastards!" Everybody laughed.

"I'm so proud of you, little brother," said Lars, popping caps off bottles of Bud for the boys. "You know who's gonna want to fuck you now? Claudia Castro."

"What!" said Dante. "You fucked Claudia Castro?"

"He hooked up with her. Didn't get it in. Am I right, J?"

Jeremy had made the mistake of bragging to his brother about making out with Claudia Castro, and now, just like his father with the Green Day contest, Lars brought it up constantly. To Lars, the Claudia Castro hook-up meant that Jeremy was making all the right choices. Positioning himself with the right people. Making the right connections and the right impressions. Lars, like most bartenders, was big on connections. Bringing people together, making things happen. His goal was to own his own bar by thirty-five. He kept everybody's business card and treated everybody as a possible investor.

"How did we not know this?" asked Dante.

"I knew," said Chris. "It was early, right? First couple days of class."

"You know who her dad is, right?" shouted Lars.

"It was just a hook-up," said Jeremy. "She was cool. We just don't really run in the same circles."

Obviously, he hadn't told anyone that he texted her half a dozen times before finally giving up. He saw her around campus sometimes, but she wasn't at the dorm much. He'd followed her on Instagram right after the hook-up and never un-followed. Her feed was mostly a cliché of cocktail glasses, skimpy tops, and manicures, but she also posted some pretty cool art. The art part annoyed him. It didn't bother him that a vapid rich girl had decided the boy from Long Island wasn't worth her time, but the fact that she had taste, that she had ideas—shouldn't she have seen that he wasn't just another freshman doofus trying to decide if he should go into law or business? He was going to be a star.

"Well, she better catch you on the way up," said Lars. " 'Cause once you're touring with Green Day I know you ain't gonna try to keep a lady at home."

Everyone agreed this was exactly right. If Claudia Castro wanted a piece of Jeremy Cahill, she better take it soon.

And, because it was the best night of his life, who should he see when they finally got to Down Under? Claudia Castro, sitting at the bar, already drunk enough that when he bellied up beside her and gave her that Green Day grin, she smiled and wrapped her arms around him for a sloppy hug.

"I know you!" she said. "See, I told you people were still around. Spring break is for *assholes*."

"Claudia's been drinking," said the guy next to her. Jeremy recognized him from the dorm but didn't know his name.

"We've all been drinking! Everyone here has been drinking, Chad. And we are going to continue drinking!" She motioned to the bartender, then looked at Jeremy. "What are you drinking?"

"Let's do a shot," said Jeremy.

She agreed. "Tequila? Chad, you want another shot?"

"Why not?"

"Three shots of tequila!"

The tequila was poured. Jeremy looked around for his bandmates but they'd all found friends in various corners of the bar. What a night, he thought.

"To the best night of my life," he said.

Jeremy didn't know if Claudia heard him. She drank the shot, shook her head, and then hopped off the barstool.

"Save my seat," she said, touching Jeremy's chest.

And because it was exactly that kind of night, Jeremy wrapped his arm around her waist, put his face in her neck, and whispered, "*You got it, baby.*"

When she was out of earshot, Chad said: "I'm fucking her tonight."

"Oh, yeah?"

"She's been a bitch to me for years, and tonight she's all brokenhearted and here I am, listening to her bullshit. That shit ain't free."

"I hear you."

"You could probably fuck her, too. Seriously, I don't mind sharing. And she's not gonna remember a thing. Trust me. I'll even let you go first."

"That's kinda fucked up, man." But as he said it he started

to imagine and he started to get hard. He was going fuck Claudia Castro on this perfect night after all. It was fate.

Ten days later, Jeremy was sick of thinking about Claudia Castro. He was sick of thinking about Chad and his father in the big black car. He was sick of seeing that video in his head, and he was sick of thinking about the thirty-thousand dollars he couldn't make happen. He wanted to think about music, he was *trying* to think about music. He was trying to get inspired. When he turned into the Mews that last night of the first part of his life, he was headed to see a professor and then to the dorm to drop off his guitar before catching the late train back to Long Island. He was walking slowly, trying to lose himself in the surround sound of his $300 headphones, twiddling his fingers with Slash to the opening bars of "Sweet Child of Mine," when what the cops told him later was probably a baseball bat came down against his skull.

TREVOR

It had seemed like something he could do when they talked about it in the hotel room. She told Trevor she paid cash for the bat and the gloves and the duffle at the Astor Place Kmart, and got the NYU cap from the store on Broadway.

"You went down to campus?" he asked, trying the cap on. It was a little small.

"I got there right when they opened. Nobody saw me. I was thinking it would be a good way to make sure you blend in, but cover your face a bit, too."

"That makes sense."

He adjusted the brim and imagined her in his mirrored sunglasses, looking for the sporting goods section, the hat wall. Presenting the sleepy cashier with a crisp one-hundred-dollar bill. Maybe even walking out without the change. Jeremy and Chad were the criminals, but Claudia was the one who had to sneak around. Trevor looked in the mirror. He'd set his mind to this, but when he saw himself in that stiff new purple-and-white hat, his mind sputtered. What was he doing here? He should be in class. The lecture this afternoon was scheduled to be about unions; he'd even done some of the reading about factory accidents and child labor when he couldn't sleep the night before.

"Was the Triangle Shirtwaist Factory near here?" he asked.

"The what?"

"A bunch of people died in a fire a long time ago . . ."

"I know what it is," she said. Was she talking down to him? "What made you think of that?"

"We're talking about it in one of my classes."

"Do you not want to be here?"

"What? No."

"No? You don't want to be here?"

"No, I *do* want to be here." It was the truth. He wanted to be there with her. He wanted to be the person doing this for her. *With* her. And he wouldn't tell her he was nervous. She didn't need any more burdens. He was going to be brave.

"But you're thinking about class," she said.

"I can't always help what I think of. Can you?"

This gave her pause. She sat down. "I *wish* I could. All I can think of is what happens when everyone in the world sees that video."

"Do you really think he'll send it out like that?"

"He might not, but it's out there. Ridley's seen it. Probably the goon who took your phone."

"Eric."

"Eric. And maybe Eric's buddy, and maybe his buddy. It doesn't have to be on Instagram to make the rounds. I'll never know when I'm with somebody who saw it. I have to figure out a way to live with that. It pretty much takes up all my brain space."

"Right."

"This will help, I think," she said. She stood up and walked to the window that looked out over the city. "I think it might rain tonight. Nobody's gonna think it's weird you're wearing gloves. Nobody'll even look twice."

Soon it was time to go. Claudia had come up with the plan: Sundown was at 7:45, so it would be full dark by 8:30. She sent Jeremy a text from a burner phone that purported to be from an emeritus professor who was a studio musician for Lady Gaga. *Hey man, it's Barry Lawes, sorry for the late notice but I might have a session spot opening for you. Come by the office around 8:45 and meet the gang?*

It worked perfectly. Jeremy texted back within minutes: *i'll be there!*

"Easy," she'd said, showing Trevor the phone. "We even got an exclamation mark. Fish on a fucking hook."

Trevor got to the Mews at sundown. It was raining and Claudia was right—that was a good thing. Nobody would be lingering, smoking a cigarette or having a conversation in weather like this. They'd be focused on getting where they were going. He pulled up his hoodie and walked one side of the street, then the other. He saw only three other people, all scurrying under umbrellas or bent beneath shoulders and a hat or hood, just like him. He made up a little story in his head in case he ran into anyone he knew, or if someone asked what he was doing. He'd gesture to the duffle under his shoulder and say, *Got sent on a prop run! See ya later!* The duffle was unzipped just enough for the bat to poke through. Trevor wanted to keep a hold on it; he didn't want to fumble when he saw Jeremy.

The address Claudia had given was closer to University than Fifth Avenue, so Trevor lingered under an awning near the gate there. He'd been through this little alley once or twice before. The houses along the cobblestone street—were they houses or offices?—seemed as if they belonged in a storybook, with window boxes full of flowers and heavy iron doorknockers. Quaint rectangular buildings, two floors, four windows; some red, some yellow, some white. It felt like a movie set, and in this movie the hero and the villain were clear. What Trevor was about to do to Jeremy was just the logical final scene: comeuppance. The thought settled his nerves just as he spotted Jeremy coming toward him on University. Trevor slid the bat out of the duffle and held it beside his leg as Jeremy turned into the Mews. This was going to be easy. He ran forward, raised the bat, and swung. Jeremy fell onto his knees, then collapsed, rolling off the curb and into the gutter. Trevor looked up and saw a woman rounding the block from Fifth. Jeremy groaned quietly, but didn't move. Had the woman seen? Was she on her phone? Jeremy's headphones were lying in a puddle beside his phone. The woman was getting nearer. He grabbed the phone and ran, jogging two blocks to the edge of Washington Square Park with the bat still in his hand. He heard no shouting, no footsteps. The sidewalk was crowded with people passing, but no one paid him any attention. An athlete late for practice. Trevor spotted a bench and sat down, further soaking his pants. He put the bat in the duffle and shoved it underneath with his feet. No sirens, no second looks, just his heart like a firecracker knocking against his ribs. He took a deep breath, and then another, and then another. He forced himself to think. He had to ditch the bat. Trevor stood abruptly, started walking, then stopped short and ran back for the duffle. He was going to make a mistake soon. *Get out of the park.* He walked toward the library; it was in the opposite direction from his dorm, but also from the alley. Half the street was closed due to construction; cars honked in the wet, their headlights lurching at his legs. At the corner of West Fourth, water flowed into an open storm drain. He slid the bat from the bag and dropped it and the phone down, watching a moment to make sure they disappeared. He continued east, thinking he'd take the long way home. The empty bag he shed a few blocks south, into one of several dumpsters outside Kmart. The gloves went into a trash can along Broadway, and the hat into another on Fourteenth Street. His ID was in his back pocket and he swiped in through the turnstiles inside the dorm. Almost everyone waiting for the elevators up was soaking wet, too. No one said a word.

He peeled off his clothes and got straight into bed. He was sober but the room spun when he shut his eyes. Trevor imagined the bat and phone traveling beneath the city, twirling inside enormous municipal pipes. Would the water destroy the phone? Should he have smashed it first? Would the bat get stuck somewhere? Would it cause a clog that backed up and up until the pressure exploded and blew open a manhole cover, or part of a sidewalk? Or would it run all the way out to the ocean? Would it float past the Statue of Liberty, like he and Claudia had? Would it wash up at Coney Island? He heard voices outside his bedroom door. What would he do if he had to talk to Boyd or one of his other roommates? Would he even be able to move his mouth? He pulled out the phone Claudia bought for him and texted Boyd: *i've got a cold. in for the night.*

A few seconds later Boyd texted back with two emojis: a thumbs-up and a mask.

When he woke up the next morning, there was an NYU Safety Alert in his email. But this time, it wasn't about the Subway Slasher:

POLICE INVESTIGATION IN WASHINGTON MEWS

> Last night the NYU Department of Safety received a report that an NYU student was found unconscious outside the French Institute at approximately 9pm. Paramedics took the student to Bellevue, where he was admitted and is in critical condition with what the hospital described as "head injuries."
>
> A report was made to the NYPD.

The NYPD. His eyes went blurry, and black spots of fear erupted inside of him, bubbling poison in a cauldron. He stood up and realized he could feel last night in his muscles. He could feel the shape of the bat in his hands. His neck hurt. His stomach. How could he have been so stupid?

Boyd was lying on the sofa when Trevor came out of his bedroom.

"You didn't have to sleep out here," said Trevor.

"Stay away," said Boyd. "I've got dress rehearsals next week and I cannot get sick."

"Got it," said Trevor. He went into the bathroom and shut the door. He peed and washed his hands and kept his eyes out of the mirror.

"Sorry, was that rude?" said Boyd when he came out. "Obviously it was rude. Can I get you something? Tea? Sudafed?"

"I'm good," said Trevor.

"Well, you look like shit."

Before he could say thank you, someone knocked at the door. Trevor opened it and found a man his father's age, sweating and red-faced.

"Is Sumit here?"

Sumit was one of their suitemates. He was from Queens and spent a lot of weekends at home.

"I don't think so," said Trevor. He turned to Boyd.

"Is everything okay?" asked Boyd.

"Jeremy's roommate said that Sumit might have his laptop." The man was breathing as if he'd been running. "We're looking for his laptop."

"Whose laptop?"

"Jeremy's!"

"Are you okay? Why don't you ask Jeremy?"

"Because he's in a coma!"

Boyd did not expect this. "Oh my God, really?"

"Yes, really. I'm his father and I need his laptop. His laptop is where all his music is. Everything he's composed since . . ." The man started coughing. No, crying. Trevor wanted to run. To his bed, out the door. Anywhere but here in the nucleus of what he'd done.

Boyd knocked on the door of the bedroom Sumit shared with their other suitemate, Corey. No answer; Boyd pushed the door open and disappeared inside. Jeremy's father wiped his face with the sleeve of his jacket.

"I'm sorry," he said, sighing heavily. He took his glasses off and rubbed his eyes. "It's an Apple. Silver, I think. It was his graduation present. I can't believe this. He was supposed to come help me with the gutters. I just thought he'd missed the train. And then I get a call in the middle of the night from the hospital."

Boyd returned. "Sumit's not in his bed, and I don't see a laptop."

"Do you know Jeremy?" asked the man.

"Not well," said Boyd. Trevor let his answer be for both of them.

"He's been meeting a lot of new people since the contest. Music industry people. I don't know any of them. I know that's normal. My dad didn't know all my friends when I was his age. Jeremy always had different groups of friends. The jocks and the punks, you know. He liked everybody. He didn't discriminate."

The man trembled as he spoke and Trevor understood that attacking Jeremy wasn't just attacking Jeremy. When police had thrown Mike and Trevor into cells in Canton, they'd locked the boys' parents up, too. What had Trevor's mom and dad said to their church friends after both their sons were arrested for selling drugs? When the other parents glared at them? When the cops interviewed them? Were Mike and Trevor part of a gang? Did they own firearms? His mom and dad had been walking with their heads down ever since. But Trevor had escaped. The essay that got him into NYU was about deciding to become a lawyer after a "cousin" went to prison. He'd written that he saw how "unjust the justice system was" to people without connections and wealth. He didn't like to think of it this way but, in a sense, Mike getting locked up gave Trevor a new life. And this is what he'd done with it. What was he going to tell his parents? Why had he thought this would help anything? Claudia didn't need this. She didn't need a lackey; she needed a friend. If he really cared about her, he had to stop her.

RIDLEY

The moment after his son showed him that stupid video, Ridley Drake began collecting evidence. If Claudia cried rape, her name alone would get her a meeting with an ADA. And once an ADA saw it—well, a certain kind of ADA; a woman—the video was a big problem. Chad was the perfect target. No one would feel sorry for his son. The tabloids would make him into a mini-Weinstein: the prep school predator. Like the Stanford swimmer but so evil that he'd recorded the whole thing. Chad would become a symbol of all that was wrong in America. Ridley had to get his hands on every copy and he had to destroy them. But he couldn't find Claudia. So he started with the boyfriend: Trevor Barber of fucking Canton, Ohio. The sister, Edie, was slumming it, too. Knocked up by some kid from Poughkeepsie. Married at twenty-three. They took after their father, he guessed.

Men like Gabe Castro were among Ridley's least favorite. So-called artists. Boot strappers. Resentful and entitled. Fifty-year-old men who wore T-shirts to board meetings. Who were they trying to kid? Michelle finally seemed to have tired of it. He'd been genuinely surprised when she flirted with him the summer before at the club, but the more he thought about it the more it made sense. Michelle Whitehouse had run the rock and roll rebel dream all the way out, and it was time to come home. Too late to play mom, he guessed, but not too late to have a second act in the world she'd rejected as a teenager.

Ridley scrolled through the names and faces on the Ohio Bar Association website and found a young woman who looked like she might be willing to do some digging. He emailed her, so she'd have time to Google and find all the handsome photos of him at microphones, celebrating with clients, leading meetings, accepting awards. Soon enough the phone rang and he spun the tale of the boy who was dating his "very naïve" niece.

"Her mother thinks she is giving him money," he said. "If you could just lift the hood a little, see if there's anything I should know about. I'd certainly owe you a night on the town. Are you ever in New York?"

The lady lawyer laughed and said she might have to plan a trip. The next day she called back with the news that Trevor Barber had a sealed juvenile record, a brother who'd served time in prison for drugs, and parents with an underwater mortgage. Twenty thousand should have been more than enough but apparently Claudia had Trevor under her spell, too. Having Eric grab the phone was risky—it upped the ante—but he'd had to make a quick decision. The boy was stupid to have turned down the money.

If he could have avoided Jeremy Cahill he would have, but Ridley needed to know if the kid from Long Island was going to be a problem. After he procured Trevor's phone, Ridley went back downtown and found Jeremy outside the dorm. He invited him into the car, and when he showed the boy the video the poor kid's face went white. After a long silence Jeremy said quietly: "That's not how I remember it."

"Well," said Ridley, "I assume there was a good bit of alcohol involved. Perhaps other substances?"

Jeremy nodded and Ridley explained that what was on the video was a crime Jeremy could do time in prison for, and that it would be best for everyone—including Claudia, because who wants to be seen like that?—if all copies were destroyed.

"I'll give you thirty thousand dollars cash if you can bring me Claudia's phone," he said.

"You can't get it?"

"I'm working on it," said Ridley, taking care not to sound irritated that he hadn't been able to track down a nineteen-year-old girl whose mother he was fucking. Though that was over now, of course.

Ridley opened his briefcase and took out an envelope.

"This is a thousand dollars," he said to Jeremy. "Take it. If you get the phone, call the number on the card inside."

He supposed he hadn't really expected the kid to deliver

but neither had he expected the call he got a few mornings later from Chad, saying that Jeremy was in the hospital.

"He got jumped or something last night," said his son over the phone.

In the car on the way to Bellevue, Ridley called a friend at the NYPD.

"My son and his friends are concerned," he said. "Do you think it was random? Targeted?"

"The surveillance cameras in the Mews weren't functional, so we don't know much," said the friend, a lieutenant. "Kid's got a fractured skull and a ruptured eardrum. Blunt object probably but we haven't found anything. Guy took his phone but not his wallet. If I had to guess I'd say some homeless off his meds or high. We've had a few muggings this semester. Nothing this bad, though."

At the information desk Ridley was told that Jeremy was on the second floor in intensive care. Ridley despised hospitals. Every molecule coated with sickness. If he could have donned a hazmat suit without looking like a lunatic, he would've. He let someone else press "2" then held his hands beneath a hand sanitizer station in the hall, rubbed the slimy bubbles over his skin, and elbowed open the swinging doors to the unoccupied nurse's station. Room 211 was at the end of a hall, the door slightly open. He knocked.

"Come in," croaked a male voice.

Jeremy lay in the bed, his head wrapped in a helmet of white gauze. The man sitting in the chair looked mid-twenties. A brother, perhaps? He wore khaki pants and a red polo shirt, indicating a job at Verizon. Both knees popped like asynchronous pistons.

"I'm sorry to disturb you," said Ridley. "My son is friends with Jeremy. He said everyone in the dorm is really worried. I'm an attorney and I thought I could be of service."

"I'm Jeremy's brother, Lars."

"Do you know what happened?" asked Ridley.

Lars shook his head. "The police are useless."

It was a hell of a coincidence: The other boy in the video gets attacked and Claudia is suddenly MIA. He knew from Michelle that she'd missed the birth of Edie's baby. Where was she? He couldn't imagine her actually wielding whatever weapon had dropped this kid, but he could imagine her paying someone to. Maybe she didn't even need to pay. Chad was committing felonies for her pussy for free.

"We'll probably sue the school," said Lars. "It was on their property. You that kind of lawyer?"

"I am."

"My brother was about to get a *record deal*. We're talking future earnings in the millions, okay? Tens of millions. Maybe more. And now doctors say he'll never hear out of his right ear. And that's just the damage they know about now. His *brain* is swollen. Where was campus security? Where were the fucking cameras?"

"I'd say you definitely have a case."

Ridley gave the young man his card and the next day Lars called.

"My brother woke up," Lars told him. "He told me who you and your son are. I want to talk."

Lars said to meet him at the southeast corner of Bryant Park that evening. There was a Verizon store two blocks away. Ridley pulled up thirty minutes before their appointed time, and when Lars came pushing through the glass doors, Ridley rolled down the window and called his name.

"Why don't we talk in my car?" said Ridley.

Lars leaned in and looked at Ridley's driver: "I don't know that guy."

"It's not a problem," said Ridley.

Lars stepped back, shook his head.

"Son, I have something to show you."

"I'm not your son," said Lars. "And I know all about the video. Jeremy woke up and told me everything."

"Please, get in the car. It doesn't make sense to discuss this in public." The sidewalks were two lanes of bodies and backpacks and briefcases.

"I know a place in the park that's quiet," said Lars.

"I don't have a lot of time."

Lars relented and climbed inside. "Jeremy said you offered him forty thousand dollars for Claudia Castro's phone."

Ridley decided not to correct him. He wondered which brother added the ten grand.

"Why can't you find her yourself?" asked Lars.

"I'm working on it. Having an NYU ID gave your brother an advantage."

"Is that what you think? I wouldn't call him very advantaged right now."

"No," said Ridley. "You're right."

"The way I see it, you sending my brother—a fucking *teenager*—after Claudia Castro might very well be the reason he's in the hospital right now."

Was Lars trying to scare him? Small-time hustlers were exhausting.

"Look," said Ridley, "I didn't force your brother to do anything. I offered him a lot of money to do something in his own self-interest. He didn't want the police to see that video. This is the post–Me Too era, son. You can't get away with that shit anymore, especially not if you're stupid enough to get it on video. That video guarantees a conviction. Your brother understood that. I don't think he'd do well in prison. And especially now, with his limitations . . ." He let the word linger in the air. When Lars didn't bite back, he continued. "That's why he was looking for Claudia."

Lars set his face like he was ready to argue but Ridley could tell he was listening.

"Okay," said Lars, finally. "You got any leads, at least?"

Ridley took his phone from his jacket pocket, scrolled to the ID photo of Trevor that Chad had sent him from the NYU system, and handed the device to Lars.

"She's been spending a lot of time with this kid."

CHAD

The video—shooting it and sending it—was a bad idea. He could admit that. But his father's reaction was out of whack, as usual. In the package room at The Park View, Ridley asked him why the boy on the other side of the door had punched him.

"Because he found out his girlfriend's a slut," said Chad.

"That's not an answer, Chad. How are you involved?"

"I sent him a video of her sucking me off."

"Why would you do that?"

"Because it was funny."

That wasn't the reason, of course. It *was* kind of funny—Claudia Castro getting it from both ends, so out of it she pissed herself in his bed. But really, he did it because he hated her and he wanted her to suffer forever. Before she kissed him that first week at NYU, he thought he'd gotten over her. He'd spent the last two years of high school in Los Angeles with his mom, away from Claudia and away from his father's insane sex life. *How can a kid like you not get laid?* his father would ask, sometimes in front of the women he brought home. After the separation, Ridley had a woman in his bed at least three nights a week. In the morning they were always half-dressed and playing wifey, offering to make breakfast in the kitchen his mother had never used. Did they think his dad was going to marry them if they whipped up a Belgian waffle? Ridley loved it, though. He had asked Irina, the housekeeper, to make sure there were always fresh pastries in the morning, and coffee service. Chad's dad wasn't the typical fuck-and-run; he liked playing house, too. The sex was better, he once told Chad, if they think they have a chance. *A chance for what?* Chad had asked. *A chance to get all this.*

Chad started skipping breakfast but he couldn't avoid the women entirely, especially once sophomore year was over for the summer and he didn't have school to go to. They always asked the same question: *Do you have a girlfriend?* No, he didn't have a fucking girlfriend

"He hates it when people ask that," his father said once. "I don't know why," Ridley continued. "He's a good-looking kid."

"Dad."

"I'm just saying, you need to get it done. You can't go to college a virgin, Chad."

"*Dad.*"

"He's hung up on this one girl."

"Ahh," said the woman. She was a cliché in every possible way. Blond and skinny, wearing one of his father's shirts with no bra beneath, bare legs crossed at the breakfast table on the balcony overlooking Central Park. "That's sweet."

Chad wanted to throw something at her. Instead, that night he called his mom and asked if he could come live with her in Beverly Hills. Her parents were so excited she'd finally left his dad they said they'd buy her a house if she moved back. He got to California in time to try out for basketball, so in addition to being the new kid from New York he was the starting forward on a division-ranked team. Nobody knew he was a virgin who'd spent a year obsessing over the same girl. His teammates took him to house parties and just before Thanksgiving a friend said he heard that Mia Gregory, a frizzy-haired, flat-chested cheerleader whose dad owned car dealerships all over Southern California, liked him.

"I bet she'll let you fuck her if you take her to winter formal," said the friend.

Chad asked and Mia said yes and the week before the dance she gave him a blow job at a party. They went to formal as a group. Nine couples in a rented party bus, then a sleepover at someone's house. They had a bedroom to themselves and he brought a condom. She brought one, too, and she didn't ask him if he'd done this before. He kept his eyes closed and thought of Claudia. Like he always did. Mia was the ugliest girl in the group and it pissed him off that she was all he could get, even three thousand miles away from Manhattan. What was with these bitches?

For a couple of months Mia didn't complain that he didn't hold her hand at school or call her his girlfriend, and she seemed happy, or at least available, to have sex whenever he texted. She let him try pretty much anything he wanted if he pushed a little bit, and the stories he told impressed his new friends. Mia went with her family to Hawaii for spring break and back at home one of her friends, Bella, made a big show of flirting with Chad at a party. They made out in the hot tub and had sex two nights later in Bella's family's pool house. Bella was a step up and seemed game to continue what they'd started—as long as he wasn't doing it with Mia, too. When Mia came back and heard, she didn't make a scene. He ignored her and she him. The next year, as managing editor of the senior yearbook, Mia managed to get "Playing with his small dick" printed between "Varsity Basketball" and "Mock Trial" among Chad Drake's school activities. Ha ha. Fuck them all. He was going back to New York. And for the summer before he started at NYU Chad and his dad actually got along. Ridley had left his big law firm and gone on his own since the divorce. If you were worth more than twenty million dollars, you probably had him on retainer. If your daughter was caught drunk driving in the Hamptons, Ridley could get the locals to drop the charges; if the towel boy at the club was threatening to tell your wife you let him blow you, Ridley gave him money and made him sign an NDA, then got him fired. Underage girls, rape charges, domestic violence, drugs, tax fraud. The day Trevor ambushed Chad, Ridley had been coming from the courthouse where he'd just gotten a judge to sign off on probation and a fine for a CEO who'd sent a prostitute to the emergency room after a hotel encounter. The hotel had the CEO on surveillance entering the room with the girl, but Ridley got the girl's roommate to make a statement saying the prostitute had told her she was going to "jam up a suit" and get rich.

"What do you mean it was funny?" demanded Ridley in their building's package room. "Why are the police here?"

"He's the one who punched me!"

"Show me this video."

"Dad . . ."

"Show me the fucking video, Chad."

Chad handed over his phone. He watched his father, and when it got to the part where she peed, Chad snickered.

"This is Claudia Castro," said Ridley.

"Yeah."

"What is the matter with you?" he hissed.

"What?"

"You showed this to that kid out there?"

"I sent it to him. Him and Claudia and her ex."

Ridley was silent for a few seconds. "We're going to go out there and tell the cops this was all big misunderstanding, and we're going to apologize for wasting their time."

"Dad . . ."

Ridley grabbed him by the arm. "You will say nothing. Got it. Keep your mouth shut. Can you do that?"

Upstairs, after the cops left, Chad's father let loose.

"How did you get so fucking stupid?" he screamed as soon as the elevator doors closed on their penthouse. Chad tried to escape to his bedroom, but Ridley followed him up the stairs, going on and on about all the ways the video could fuck up their lives. "Do you *want* to go to prison?"

Chad kept walking. Ridley pushed him and he stumbled forward, falling briefly then popping back up, surprised and angry.

"What's the big deal? It's just a sex tape."

Ridley stared at his son for a moment. Chad had seen the same expression on his father's face last month when he told him he hadn't gotten the internship with the Brooklyn Nets.

"What happened?" Ridley had asked.

"It was between two of us and they chose the other guy. I think his dad's a state senator."

Ridley had shaken his head and looked at Chad like he'd just sung off-key. "At some point you need to start figuring out how to close the deal, son."

He'd closed the deal with Claudia, though, hadn't he? He hadn't kidnapped her. She'd come up in the elevator with him. She knew what was going to happen. She'd known it was coming. It had been coming for a long time.

"Give me your phone."

"No." Chad touched the device in his back pocket.

Ridley shook his head. Disappointed.

"Give it to me."

"I'm not giving you my phone."

Ridley stepped forward and Chad took off down the hall, sprinting into his bedroom, flipping the lock. His father kicked the door.

"I'm trying to help you, you moron!"

"I don't need your help!"

His dad was not going to back off, so he decided to wipe the phone. His contacts were in the cloud and everything else was in apps he could log back into. He could probably even find the video if he really wanted to. But he didn't need it, he thought, as he Googled "erase contents of iPhone"—he'd been there.

When he finally opened the bedroom door, his father was still standing there. Chad pushed the phone into his chest and walked past him, headed down the stairs to the elevator.

"What did you do, Chad?"

"Fuck you, Dad."

And that should have been the end of it.

CLAUDIA

Lesley showed up late, but looked exactly right. Short black dress, high heels, cleavage, big hair, glossy lips. The full cliché.

"You look great," said Claudia.

"Yeah?" Lesley found the mirror on the wall and checked, running her hand along her hair, turning to check out her ass. "Good. Obviously he's into you, but does that mean your *look*? His Instagram had him with more basic bitches. So I went that way."

"It's perfect. He'll probably nut at the bar."

"Damn," said Lesley. She sat down on the sofa and pulled a baggie out of her purse. "That's an image."

Claudia laughed. She liked who she was with Lesley. With Lesley, Claudia was in charge. She was strong again, capable. Could she keep that up with Chad in the room?

Lesley laid two lines of white powder on the coffee table, took a pad of yellow Post-its from her purse, and rolled a straw.

"One for you?" she offered.

"I'm good."

Lesley shrugged and snorted.

"It's just coke. The other thing's in a little dropper." She wiped her nose then got up and went into the bathroom. Claudia heard the water running.

"I was thinking," called Lesley, "maybe you should just give me the rest of the money now."

Knock knock.

Claudia went to the door and saw Trevor through the peephole. He wasn't supposed to be here. The plan had been to keep everything offline and connect in a couple days. She didn't want him to meet Lesley. All this felt manageable if she kept things simple. Two people in a room at a time. Everybody on a need-to-know.

She opened the door.

"What are you doing here?"

He pushed past her.

"Is Chad here?"

"What? No."

"Good."

Trevor started jabbering about Jeremy's dad, but Claudia interrupted him.

"Stop talking," she said. "Did something happen?"

"Yes, something happened!"

Lesley came out of the bathroom. "Who's this?"

Trevor grabbed Claudia's wrist. She shook him off.

"I need to talk to you," he said.

"You are talking."

"Claudia, who is this guy?"

"Don't worry. We go to school together."

"Tell him he better not fucking touch you again," said Lesley.

"I'm fine," said Claudia. "He's harmless. *Thank you.* Why don't you head down to the bar?"

"Whatever you say," said Lesley. She picked her purse up off the bed and left with a little kick of her heel. The clock beside the bed said 9:15 p.m.

"Did you do it?" asked Claudia when Lesley was gone.

"Sort of."

"What do you mean?"

"He's in the hospital."

"Did you get his hands?" The plan had been to knock him down with a blow to the head, then smash his fingers. No fingers, no guitar god.

"I couldn't do that part," said Trevor. "His brain is swollen, he's . . ."

"Can he still play the guitar?"

"Claudia, listen to me. You need to call this off. Whatever you're going to do to Chad, I don't think you should do it. I think you'll regret it."

She drew a sharp breath. "Oh, really?"

"I know you will."

"Oh, you *know* I will?" The confidence she felt alone in the room with Lesley had vanished. She didn't have the strength to argue with Trevor for long.

"I met his dad," Trevor said. "He's freaking out. Jeremy's really fucked up."

"That was the point. As you know."

"I just don't think you want to do this. I mean, I don't think you want to *have* done it. You don't want this on your conscience. It's not right."

"Of course it's not *right*, you asshole!" she screamed. "None of this is *right*! They did this. This is on them."

"I think you'll regret it," he almost whispered. "What if you get caught?"

Claudia stared at him, her eyes flashing. Was he really doing this to her? A million words came rushing into her mouth but she wasn't going to say any of them. She wasn't going to explain herself. She wasn't going to spend another ounce of energy on this fucking traitor.

"Fuck off, Trevor," she said finally.

"Claudia—"

"Bye."

Claudia pushed him into the hall and slammed the door shut. Fury rose and radiated inside her. She grabbed a pillow and pressed it to her face, screaming so hard her throat burned with the effort. Deep breath, then again. The scream roared and scratched, like the rage that spawned it was clawing through the muscle and bone and skin. She wiped her leaking face with the pillow and threw it at the window. Fourteen floors below, the city was moving. Lights flashing a party every square inch. She imagined herself pushed into a cab: *Come on, Claudia, what's wrong? It'll be fun, Claudia. It's a party, Claudia. Everybody knows you like parties.* She filled up a glass of water at the bathroom sink and drank it with her eyes closed. She picked up her toothbrush and her pills, looked around to make sure she hadn't left anything else, and put them in the zipper pocket inside the duffle. Two thousand dollars for a go-bag. Why had she bought this ridiculous thing? Because for a few moments in Macy's, surrounded by designer bags, she'd been able to recapture the ease of her life before: pick an item, charge it, take it home, enjoy it, show it off. It wasn't happiness but it was, she understood now, power. Power she wanted back.

There was a convenience store opposite the bar in the hotel lobby, and the plan was for Lesley to drink a round, order another, then ask Chad to go buy a couple mini-bottles of Jack Daniel's so they could "take the party" to her room. While he was gone, she'd drop the drug in his drink. Lesley said that her guy said the ketamine would take about twenty minutes to kick in, and Claudia's Googling found the same thing. Three drops, apparently. So, when Chad brought back the mini-bottles she'd tell him to drink up and settle the check.

At just after ten, Lesley texted that they were headed up. Claudia slid the mirrored closet door open and got into place, wedged beside the wall-mounted iron, hangers inches from her forehead, the Louis Vuitton at her feet. She waited, and after a few minutes heard the *beep* and *click* of the door opening.

"Not bad for a Holiday Inn," said Chad.

"Snob," Lesley teased. They were inches from the closet mirror.

"Next time I'll take you someplace really nice," he slurred.

"Will you? You're so sexy."

Kissing.

"Mm, you taste good," said Lesley. Claudia could smell his cologne. "I'll open the Jack, you get on the bed. I've got ideas."

"Ideas, huh?"

"Promise you won't tell anybody?"

"Promise."

"I did some strippin' back in Atlanta. You want a little show?"

"Oh, yeah," said Chad. Claudia wished she could see his face. She imagined his slavering smile. Thinking: *How'd I get so lucky?*

"Just lie down. Let me take care of you."

She heard Lesley unscrew the bottles and pour their contents into glasses. Footsteps.

"Hey," said Lesley. "Hey. You awake? You awake?"

A moment later the mirrored door opened.

"He's all yours."

Claudia stepped out and there was Chad Drake, lying on the bed. One shoe on, one shoe off. His oxford tucked into dark jeans. A leather belt, a clean white undershirt, a watch she knew cost thousands of dollars.

"How would you feel about me taking that watch?" asked Lesley.

"Are you sure he's out?"

"Go check if you want."

Claudia walked to the edge of the bed. "Chad? Chad?" She shook his socked foot. Shook it harder. Then she poked his chest. He was out.

"Take it," she said.

Lesley wasted no time, and as she unhooked her bonus, Claudia got the envelope of cash from the duffle bag.

"Where are you headed?" she asked Lesley as she handed over the money.

"I figure it's best to get out of the city for a little bit," said Lesley. "Perfect time for a vacation."

"What about your job?"

"Hooters? My boss is cool. There's a million girls that can cover my shifts."

They agreed to delete each other from their phones and said goodbye.

"Be careful," said Lesley as she left.

"You, too."

This time Claudia didn't slam the door. She closed it quietly and paused looking at the extra bolt. She didn't need to keep danger out, it was already inside. If anything, she'd need an easy exit. Her first idea had been to do something Chad would consider sexually humiliating. Maybe take a picture of his flaccid dick and tag it with his name so that whenever you Googled "Chad Drake," that was what popped up; or make a video of him getting blown by a male prostitute. But none of that seemed exactly right. She never seriously entertained the idea of killing him. What would that even look like? *Gone Girl*? Then run screaming down the hotel hallway: *He raped me! He raped me!* Who would she run to? She wasn't a murderer. But it was time for Chad to be a victim. Finally, scrolling through her phone last night, unable to sleep, Claudia saw the words that made it click: *Another Victim: Slasher attacks from behind.* That's it, she thought: I'll cut him.

In the morning she went in search of an instrument. There were steak knives in the kitchenette but when she ran them along her fingertips they were dull. She knew she'd have to do it quickly; she couldn't trust that whatever Lesley dropped in Chad's drink would last through much dithering. The news said the Slasher was probably using a box cutter, so she walked down to Fourteenth Street and found one at the Home Depot. The clerk barely looked at her. Back in the room, she Googled "How to tell if your knife is sharp," and tested the blade on a piece of the hotel stationary. It slid straight through.

Claudia took the box cutter out of her bag. She peered over Chad, just lying there, breathing. She studied his face; his gaping pores and puffy nose. He still bit his fingernails, she could see. She imagined him grinning, chewing at a hand, sending the video to group chat after group chat, accompanied, perhaps, by some crude gif. Or maybe just what he'd written to Trevor: *Claudia Castro is a slut.* Chad Drake was a monster and it was time everyone knew that.

She slid the box cutter's blade up.

"If you can hear me," she said, leaning over him, "I hope this hurts."

She took a shallow breath and drew the edge along his cheekbone. He stirred and she jumped back. The blood ran down both sides of his face, neck to ear, and onto his lips. He jerked up, sputtered, then slumped back. She looked down at her hands: They were clean. They were steady. Chad began to moan. He put his hand to his face and the blood ran through his fingers, tucked into his raggedy cuticles. Their eyes met and she flipped him off.

If Chad said anything, Claudia didn't hear it. She put the box cutter into a plastic bag she'd prepped in the duffle, left the room and walked out of the hotel toward the Port Authority.

Claudia moved through Midtown easily, weaving between groups of pedestrians, judging the speed of approaching vehicles as she came upon an intersection, navigating outdoor dining setups and orange construction cones and falafel carts as if she were the human character in some virtual chase game. How fast can you get the girl from the hotel to the bus station through the after-theater rush? She liked that Chad had seen her. She liked that she was moving forward, literally speeding away from him, and his nightmare was just beginning.

LARS

Before he got out of the car, Ridley Drake texted Lars the photo of Trevor Barber. Jeremy said he thought the kid was in his dorm, so Lars took off work and for the next two days he hung out on the corner of Fourteenth Street and Broadway, watching the three revolving entrance doors. Thank God for the bathroom in Starbucks. At first it felt like an impossible task: He had one photo of a brown-haired kid with no terribly distinguishing features. But after just a few minutes he realized that white males were few and far between. It was mostly Asians and women. He smirked when he realized it. Of course his brother and Trevor were the minorities at schools like NYU. He wondered what remarkable thing Trevor had done to get in. Or maybe his parents were alums. Finally, just as Lars was starting to think about getting a gyro from a corner cart for dinner on day two, Trevor emerged.

Lars followed him west, then north, ten blocks, twenty, thirty, and eventually up the walkway to a Holiday Inn on Fifty-Seventh Street. The lobby was crowded with guests but Trevor weaved straight through them to the elevators. Lars had to make a quick decision: Get on with him? He decided yes. They'd never met and the chances of Trevor seeing a resemblance with Jeremy, from a passing glance, were negligible. He got on, along with a white-haired woman who smelled strongly of lipstick and a couple in matching windbreakers, speaking a language he didn't understand. Russian? French? Lars followed Trevor off at the eighth floor, his phone out, ready to claim he was lost if necessary. He stayed several steps behind, but Trevor didn't look back once before knocking on a door at the end of the hall. Lars heard a girl's voice: "What are you doing here?"

It had to be Claudia. But he wasn't going to get her phone with this kid—and whoever else was in the room—protecting her. Eventually she'd leave. And when she did he'd be in the lobby. He took the elevator back down and found a spot to wait.

Twenty minutes later Trevor emerged looking despondent, moving slowly toward the exit. Maybe she dumped him, Lars thought. Crazy bitch. He's better off. Lars leaned against a four-foot ceramic pot holding bamboo shoots for an hour. Eventually, he moved to the bar on the other side of the lobby, taking the last remaining seat between a woman with dreadlocks wearing a cheap job-search pants suit, and a couple starting to get handsy. The guy looked vaguely familiar, but Lars had seen so many faces working bars over the years that he just figured he'd served him once. From his stool he could see the elevators.

"Double bourbon and a Bud back," he told the bartender.

"Start a tab?"

"No," he said. "I'll probably be headed out soon. Just waiting on a text."

The bartender brought the drinks and Lars gave him one of the hundred-dollar bills from Ridley's envelope. One thousand dollars of what the slick attorney had called "good faith" money. He slammed the bourbon, and the beer didn't last as long as he'd hoped, so he ordered another.

He was on his third when Claudia came out of the elevator and nearly ran across the lobby. He left his beer and the change and went after her, his heart racing. It was like chasing a bag of money: *Do not let it out of your sight*, he thought. He followed her into the swarm of voices and horns and lights on Fifty-Seventh. She crossed Eighth and turned south, walking fast, an enormous Louis Vuitton bag slung over her shoulder. That bag probably cost five thousand dollars. That bag could pay Jen the back child support he owed. He'd actually bought his ex the $300 starter model when they first hooked up. She liked it so much she started shoplifting bigger ones from Roosevelt Field mall.

"You created a monster!" she'd joked as she showed off her loot back at her mom's house. She was always in a great mood after she got one and she always wanted to fuck.

They were both living with their parents when they hooked up. Both about to start at Stony Brook, planning to major in business. Her dad was an accountant and, according to Jen, squeezed her mom and her out of what they deserved when he left to make another family.

"Jeni inherited his head for numbers," her mom, Karen, told him the first time they met. They were at a pizza parlor where sirens rang to announce a customer's birthday. "And they're both Leos. So you can see what I'm up against."

Lars had no idea what she meant, but he didn't say that. He was nineteen then and knew enough to know that it was important to get in good with your girl's mom. Not too good, though; Karen was the kind who would make a pass at you. He'd fielded several in high school. His mom was not that kind of mom. His mom was older, fragile, sexless, with her prematurely gray hair always in a braid, her flat dancer's chest, her big feet. Lars loved that Jen dressed up sexy for him—well, for a while it was for him. He'd bought her that stupid purse to encourage her, and to telegraph that he saw himself as someone who could one day afford to buy her lots of things like that. Because he knew that's what she wanted. Wasn't it what they all wanted? And he did expect to have money, vaguely. He'd started bar-backing at a local steak house at eighteen and was writing the cocktail menu by twenty-two. The loose plan was to keep on tending bar, get to know the distributors, start working sales, then maybe open his own place with seed money from some of his rich high school buddies by the time he was thirty.

But that hadn't happened. He got his associate's, and an entry level job at Seagram's, but the combination of a job involving alcohol and an increasingly volatile romantic relationship was toxic. He started missing morning appointments. Jen put him through the ringer. She was a talker. Every little thing, every disagreement, they had to have it out. Round after round all night long in her bedroom, or on the back porch in the dark, or in one of their cars. Pleading and accusing and apologizing, over and over and over. Then a couple days of silence, of wondering if it was finally the end, then a text and a tender-dirty fuck and they were back on.

So, at twenty-four it was back to bartending; by twenty-seven he'd missed out on investing in two different bars because he couldn't come up with the ten grand when it came time. How did anybody save ten thousand dollars working behind a bar? If his mom hadn't gotten cancer he might have asked his parents for the money, but she had, and then Jen got pregnant, and he drank more, and now at twenty-eight he was back in his old bedroom in Port Jeff, working nights at the bar and days at the fucking Verizon store to pay child support just to keep out of jail. His son cried when he came to take him for their afternoons together, his former classmates posted Instagram photos of their sky-high Manhattan apartments, and every year seemed to be a new lesson in the shittiness of white male life.

And now Claudia Castro thought she could fuck with him, too. As she crossed Fiftieth Street he wondered, *Should I just tackle her*?

Times Square was so bright it felt like noon. Fat tourists clogged the sidewalks, staring up, recording videos of the lights. People performed for spare change in filthy costumes. Would that be him someday? So desperate for money he'd do anything? Beg? When Jeremy won that contest, Lars had allowed himself to think that his brother's success would be his safety net. Jeremy and Rock would record a hit record and there would be more than enough money to go around. He and his brother would go in on a bar, maybe something like the Hard Rock but owned by an actual musician. Claudia Castro stole that. She stole his brother's future and with it his future; she stole any chance his dad had at a comfortable retirement. And for what? She got drunk and got fucked like a million other girls, but this bitch thought she was special.

Lars kept walking behind her, hoping an opportunity would present itself. She took the stairs down at Forty-Second Street, but instead of swiping into the subway she followed the passageway toward Port Authority. Underground the energy was darker. It was oddly quiet; people dragged their luggage slowly and drank paper-bag beers alone. Claudia went to a kiosk and bought a ticket, though Lars couldn't see to where. He was standing ten feet behind her. She looked up to the timetable and then turned around. His heart dropped. But her eyes moved right past him to the restaurant behind. TGI Fridays. The Knicks game was on.

She sat down at the bar and put her bag on the stool next to her. The fucking feminists made such a big deal of "manspreading" that the MTA did a whole ad campaign with his tax dollars. He needed to come up with a catchy phrase to describe the way women piled all their shit around them in bars. He could make up a mug that read: "JUST SAY NO TO BITCHES' BAGGAGE." It didn't exactly flow.

Lars sat down on the stool next to her duffle. The bag was zipped shut.

"What can I get you?" the bartender asked Claudia.

"Double vodka and soda, please," she said. Her voice was soft. Lars had Googled her after Jeremy told him they hooked up last fall. Online, Claudia Castro seemed like someone he'd want to fuck, too. Petite, long dark hair, nice tits, big smile. But the girl at the bar looked nothing like the girl he'd seen online. The girl at the bar looked brittle, like a little witch.

"And you?"

The bartender was talking to him.

"Uh, Budweiser, bottle."

Claudia took her phone out of her pocket. His throat closed up. He could see the money. Forty thousand dollars, three feet away, in her small hands. Forty thousand dollars meant nothing to Claudia Castro. Claudia Castro ate forty thousand dollars for breakfast. The way he saw it, Claudia Castro owed him way more than forty thousand dollars. But it was a start.

The bartender came back with their drinks. Lars held his beer and watched Claudia in the slices of mirror behind the bottles along the back of the bar. She leaned forward, tucked into herself, and sucked the drink through the cocktail straw. When she'd drained it, she motioned for another, then pulled the ticket she'd bought from her purse.

"Do you know where this gate is?" she asked the bartender when he came back with her drink.

He leaned over. "Woods Hole? That's two levels down."

"Thanks." She tucked the ticket back into her duffle. "Could you watch this for just a minute?"

"Sure, hon," said the bartender.

Claudia slid off the barstool. She was going to the bathroom. It was now or never.

The restrooms were in a vestibule off the dining area. Lars stood just around the corner that she would have to turn to come back to the bar. Two minutes later she did just that, and he threw his shoulder into her.

It couldn't have worked better. *Wham*. She fell forward on the carpet. Her phone at her feet.

"Oh my God are you okay?" he said, kneeling, slipping the phone into his back pocket.

"Jesus!" she said, up in a nanosecond. "What the fuck?"

"I'm so sorry, I wasn't looking . . ."

"Where's my phone?"

"Your phone?"

"You took my phone!" Her voice was suddenly very loud.

"I didn't take your phone. Look, I'm sorry I accidentally . . ."

"Give me that!" She lunged at him and he jumped back.

"What the fuck!" he exclaimed.

"Everything okay over here?" It was the bartender. The people at the tables around them were looking.

"No," said Claudia. "He tripped me and now he has my phone."

"Is that true?"

"No," said Lars. "It was an accident. We bumped into each other."

"Tell him to give me my phone back."

"Sir, do you have her phone?"

"No!" His voice cracked a little.

"He's lying," she said. "Check his pocket."

"Miss . . ." said the bartender.

She looked at Lars. "Let him check your pockets," she demanded.

"Or what?" He hadn't thought this through.

The bartender put his hand on Lars's chest. "Everybody calm down."

"Don't touch me," said Lars, stepping back. "She's the one freaking out."

"Check his pockets," Claudia said again.

"Sir?"

Lars put his hands up. "I don't have her fucking phone."

"Great, then can you please just show us your pockets so we can refocus this young lady's attention?"

"You don't believe me?"

"I don't know you, man!"

"Fuck you both." Lars started to walk away, but Claudia grabbed his shirt.

"What the *fuck*!" he yelled.

"You're the one making this hard," said the bartender. "Just show her what's in your pockets."

Lars pushed the bartender and tried to run but the asshole must have had a black belt in something. He grabbed

Lars easily, neck and arms, turned him around and took the phone out of his back pocket.

"Is this yours?"

Claudia snatched it. "Yes. Thank you."

"Do you want to press charges?" asked the bartender.

She hesitated. "No."

"Are you sure?" asked the bartender, still holding Lars's arms.

She started crying. Fucking bitch.

The bartender tightened his grip on Lars.

"Go get your bus, hon," he said. "I'm really sorry. We'll take care of this asshole."

Claudia looked at Lars. Her hair was a mess. Was that blood on her cheek? And then out of nowhere, she opened her mouth and screamed. It was wet and repulsive, inches from his face. He closed his eyes against her breath. She was tiny. He could crush her. He *should* crush her. He would crush her. Or if not her, her fucking family. Somebody was going to pay.

PART 4

EDIE

The man at the door wanted to come in.

"How do you know Claudia?" asked Gabe.

From the sofa, maybe twenty feet away, Edie didn't recognize him. Twenties, probably. White. Mets cap, hoodie.

"I don't want to talk out here," he said.

"I don't know who you are," said Gabe. "I'm not just going to . . ."

The man shoved her father. Gabe tripped backward and the man closed the door behind him. Nathan jumped up and moved like he was going to grab him, but the man stepped back and raised his hands.

"I just want to have a conversation," he said. "Is Claudia here?"

"No," said Edie.

"She's still hiding?"

"Hiding? Hiding where?" asked Michelle.

"Give me one reason I shouldn't call the police right now," said Gabe.

"Because your daughter is in some deep shit."

"Who are you?" demanded Gabe.

"I'm the guy she owes fifty grand. I'm the guy whose brother she put in the hospital. And I'm the guy who's going to make your life pretty fucking miserable if you don't let me sit down and tell you what needs to happen."

"Do you know where she is?" Edie asked quietly.

"Maybe."

"When was the last time you saw her?" asked Michelle.

"I can tell you that. But not for free."

"Why would Claudia owe you fifty thousand dollars?" asked Gabe.

"Would you like me to explain?"

Edie watched her parents look at each other. They were going to say yes. They were going to invite him in. What else could they do? As he walked toward the center of the first floor and into the sunlight, the man fiddled with the bill of his Mets cap. He tugged it up and gave his head a little scratch, and that's when Edie recognized him.

"You're the other guy in the video," she said.

He paused and Edie thought she saw a hint of a smile. Or was it a sneer?

"She showed you?"

"No," said Edie, raising her voice. "None of us have seen

my sister in two weeks. She's not answering our calls. She's not online. Because of what you and Chad did to her."

"You don't know what the fuck you're talking about," said the man in the hat. "Would you like to see a photograph of what your sister did to my brother? Yeah, I think that's a good idea."

He pulled his phone out of his pocket, scrolled and clicked, then handed the device to Edie. It was a picture of someone in a hospital bed, head wrapped in white bandages.

"She attacked him. She *lured* him. The police say that when they find who did it it'll be felony assault. Maybe even attempted murder. He was in a coma. They don't think he'll ever fucking *hear* right."

"There isn't a reason in the world we should believe anything you're saying," said Gabe.

"My sister didn't *attack* anybody," said Edie. "She barely weighs a hundred pounds."

"Oh, I'm sure she paid somebody to do it. Because that's what you people do. Pay people to do shit you want done but are too pussy to do yourselves. Don't worry, whoever actually held the bat, or whatever it was, he'll get his. But right now, if you don't want me to go straight from here to the *New York Post* with the story about the psycho rich bitch who destroyed a young artist's life, you're going to give me fifty grand."

"You're not going to the newspaper," said Michelle. "If that's your brother in the video he's in as much trouble as she is."

"Not the way I see it. Jeremy is an all-American college boy. And people are getting sick of this feminist 'me too,' 'rape culture' bullshit. Your daughter is a privileged little princess who had a temper tantrum because she got too drunk and couldn't keep her legs together. And now my brother's life is ruined."

"Your brother is a rapist," said Edie.

He didn't even seem to hear her. "Just give me the fucking money and you'll never see me again."

"What about Claudia?" asked Gabe. "You said you'd tell us where she is."

"No, I said what I know about where she is would not be free. I tried to get Claudia to cooperate. Now I'm trying to get you to cooperate. If she had just given me her phone I wouldn't be here."

"What the fuck are you talking about?" screamed Edie. She stood up and went toward him. Her whole body was vibrating with fear and disgust. She wanted to claw at his face. She looked around. What could she throw? What could she do to make him tell her? "When did you see her? What did you do?"

"I didn't do shit," said the man.

"Where is my sister?"

"I don't know where your fucking sister is."

"Get out," said Gabe. "I'm calling the police."

"I told you that was a bad idea," said the man.

"I don't give a shit what you told me. I don't have a fucking clue who you are and you're in my house, threatening my family."

The man pulled a gun from beneath his waistband and pointed it at Gabe.

"My name is Lars Cahill, and you're going to put the phone down. You're going to give me the money you owe me and my family, and maybe, *maybe* we won't sue your ass for every penny you have. I know a pretty good lawyer."

Was he talking about Ridley? "Who sent you here?" whispered Michelle.

"Your fucking daughter sent me here."

Edie's dad stood frozen, eyes on the barrel of the weapon that was inches from his forehead.

"There's money in the safe," said Gabe.

They all looked at him. Edie's parents had argued about the safe for years. Her dad always wanted to keep more cash in it than her mom. Michelle believed in banks. She believed in real estate and the stock market. She was practiced at having money and she felt certain that it would always be there. Why shouldn't it? People who were afraid kept piles of cash in a safe at home. What did they have to be afraid of?

"Take me up there," said Lars, the gun still pointed at Edie's dad.

"No." Gabe looked at Edie and Nathan. Lydia was upstairs. "I'll go."

"No way, you'll call the cops."

"In ten minutes, you can walk out of this house with fifty thousand dollars in your pocket. But you have to trust me."

Lars didn't answer immediately. He adjusted his grip on the handgun.

"All I have to do is walk upstairs and get the cash," said

Gabe. "What I care about is my family. I'm not going to fuck with you while you have a gun on my family. I want this over as fast as you do."

"Three minutes," said Lars.

Gabe ran toward the stairs and Edie heard his footsteps up the first flight, then the second. Nathan gently pulled Edie toward him, and guided her body behind his. He reached out to Michelle and did the same. The three of them stood in a triangle, holding on to each other. Would this work? Gabe said the money was in the safe, but what if it wasn't? What if Lars got angry? When she was pregnant, Edie and Nathan had watched a PBS documentary about stolen babies and adoption scams. People in the U.S. are willing to pay hundreds of thousands of dollars for a light-skinned newborn. What if Lars had watched the same show? What if Lydia started crying? Where was Claudia?

"Where's Claudia?" she asked.

Her mother squeezed her arm. "Just wait."

Lars lowered his gun and Edie saw that he was trembling. Was that good or bad? If he's scared, he's unpracticed, maybe unsure about being there. Maybe that's good. He doesn't want to hurt them. But scared is careless. And careless plus gun is bad. She watched his face. Again, the smile-sneer.

"You guys have a place on Martha's Vineyard, right? She's probably up there."

Why hadn't they thought of that? Her sister loved that island. The first year Edie was gone at Vassar, Claudia tried to convince their parents to let her stay at the Edgartown house and finish high school there. Claudia wasn't the kind of kid who was always planning her future, but when she talked about "someday," it was always on the Vineyard. *Someday maybe I'll own a flower shop. Someday maybe I'll teach surfing. Someday maybe I'll open a gallery.* Of course that's where she'd gone.

"Is she okay?" asked Michelle.

Lars shrugged. "Last I saw her she had a bus ticket and was having a drink at the TGI Fridays in Port Authority."

Gabe came down the stairs with a handful of cash wrapped in the neat bundles Edie and Claudia had snooped at as kids. The paper money wasn't nearly as interesting to them as the jewelry Michelle inherited: big milky pearls; cocktail rings with knuckle-sized sapphires and emeralds; diamond necklaces, diamond bracelets, diamond earrings, a dainty diamond watch with a black silk strap. The girls would play with the jewelry for hours when their parents were gone. Lars could have had all of it if he'd been a little smarter maybe. *Fuck him*, she thought.

Lars took the money from Gabe and went to count it, but seemed to reconsider when he realized he'd have to put the gun away. He backed toward the front door. It was almost over.

"He said he saw Claudia at Port Authority," said Michelle. "She's on the Vineyard."

"How did she seem when you saw her?" asked Gabe

Lars lifted his sweatshirt and stuck the gun into the front of his pants.

"How did she seem?" he said. "She seemed like a bitch."

Edie kept the scream inside. When Lars left the house was silent. They all looked at the door. Would bullets come flying through? They did not. Gabe flipped the deadbolt. It was over. And upstairs, Lydia was crying.

"Go," said Gabe.

Edie went and so did Nathan. When they came back downstairs, Michelle was on the phone fruitlessly trying to book a charter flight to the Vineyard that evening. JetBlue was the only commercial carrier that flew from New York to the island, and in the off-season the flights were every other day. The ferry from the mainland cut off service early, too, so even if they'd gotten in the car thirty minutes ago, they wouldn't have been been able to make the last one. Edie listened as her father left a message for Dave Wilcox, the Edgartown caretaker.

"Call me back as soon as you can," said Gabe.

Edie set Lydia down on the Boppy pillow and gave the girl her finger to hold. She was supposed to be doing at least an hour of "skin to skin" with the baby every day. She was supposed to lie down, bare-chested, and place Lydia on her and they were supposed to . . . breathe? Bond? They were never going to get this time back. She sat on the sofa holding the baby and strapped the nursing pillow, like a foam lifesaver, around her waist. Her mother came in from the kitchen, breathing hard.

"I can't get us there until the morning."

"Should we call the police now?" Edie asked.

"I called Ingrid," said Michelle. "I gave her the name and she'll get back to us."

"Ingrid isn't the police," said Edie.

"She's better."

"Dad?"

"I sent you both a link," said Gabe. Michelle sat down on the sofa next to Edie and they clicked. The link was an article from the *New York Post*, published the day before:

NYU "ROCK" STAR BRUTALLY ATTACKED ON CAMPUS

By Larry Dunn

He'll never play again.

Long Island native Jeremy Cahill, 19, was set to make an album with Green Day, but the freshman's father says a "sicko" attacked him on the way to meet with a professor, shattering an eardrum and fracturing the teen's skull.

"Whoever did this is a monster," said Peter Cahill, 56.

NYPD Sgt. Wesley Swain said Cahill was assaulted around 9 p.m. Saturday night in the Washington Mews.

A police source who asked not to be named said that surveillance cameras in the area may not have been functional, and the department is actively seeking witnesses.

"His phone was gone, but whoever did it left his wallet and his backpack," said the source.

Cahill is the lead singer and guitarist for the band Rock. He grew up in Port Jefferson, NY.

Edie's hand was on Lydia's chest; it began to tingle.

"The kid was telling the truth," said Michelle.

"Some of it, at least," said Gabe.

Claudia had to be in Martha's Vineyard, thought Edie. This horrible thing had happened to her and she'd run. *I would have run, too.*

"I'm gonna call the house," Edie said. "Maybe she'll pick up."

But the phone in Edgartown just rang and rang, and the family decided that the best plan was to go to the Vineyard tomorrow and get Claudia. Whatever she'd done, they'd deal with it.

Edie guided Lydia onto her breast and the girl, possibly sensing that another frustration might actually destroy her mother, latched on easily. Edie touched her black hair and looked at the tiny white dots across her face. The pediatrician said they were normal, that they'd be gone in a couple of weeks. What else would be different in a couple of weeks? Lydia finished her meal and gave a popping burp when Edie patted her back. Nathan found a notepad in the kitchen and they started making a list of all the things they needed to bring with them to the Vineyard. The pump, the bottles, the nipples, the nursing pillow, the diapers, the wipes, the Aquaphor, the onesies, the swaddles, the little first aid kit with the thermometer and the medicine spoon and the fingernail clippers and the nose bulb. They needed bags for the milk she pumped and pads for inside her nursing top. They needed so much all of a sudden. If she wasn't so weighed down, could she have prevented this? If Edie hadn't had the baby, would Claudia have come to her instead of running away?

Dave Wilcox called back the next morning as they headed to the airport. Gabe put the call on speaker.

"I'm at the house with the police," said Dave. "There's no sign of Claudia. But a young man appears to have spent the night. He says Claudia told him he could stay."

TREVOR

The plan, before he fucked it up, had been for them to take separate busses on separate days to Claudia's family home on Martha's Vineyard and wait there together. *Until it blows over*, she'd said. It sounded reasonable at the time. But as the days passed since she'd told him to fuck off, Trevor realized that nothing that had happened was going to blow over. And none of it was reasonable. He went through the motions of class and eating but the more time that went by, the more worried he became. She hadn't explicitly said that she wanted him with her for protection, but it made sense: Everyone in her life was unavailable, untrustworthy, or both. She'd leaned on him and he'd let her down. He'd thought he'd known better than her. And now she was alone on an island—if she'd even made it there.

Trevor decided he had to act, so he packed a bag and

bought a bus ticket and on the long ride to Massachusetts he imagined all the things that could have befallen her. She could have been overpowered by Chad and disposed of by Ridley. She could have run from the room covered in blood, been grabbed by security and arrested. She could have jumped in front of a train.

After eight hours on three different busses, Trevor boarded the ferry at Woods Hole. The long, low boom of the horn startled him, and he went up onto the deck to watch the boat push off. Every brunette was Claudia. It was all a big misunderstanding. It was dark when they docked in a little town with twinkly lights and sailboats floating along the shore. Should he show up unannounced? Trevor stood beneath an overhang at the terminal and watched people get into cars; some lined up for a bus. He was nervous so he started walking uphill, toward the lights. The big grocery store was still open but employees were starting to bring bags of garbage out to the parking lot. He heard the crash of glass bottles together and it reminded him of the summer after junior year when he worked making sandwiches at a deli near City Hall. On the shifts when he helped close, they'd blast music and mop, and then he'd take the trash out to the alley where homeless people sometimes bedded down. Once he'd startled a man digging through the dumpster. The man was squatting precariously along the edge of the giant bin and when Trevor kicked the back door open he fell in. *Oh, shit*! Trevor said. *Are you okay?* He stepped on an overturned milk crate and looked down at the mass of bags, some open and leaking; rotting sandwich meat; coffee grounds; cartons of half-and-half; slimy ribbons of shredded lettuce. The man was face down and for a moment Trevor thought maybe he was dead. *Are you okay?* he repeated. After a few seconds, the man stirred; he tried to bring his knees beneath him and press his arms to push himself up, but the bags were shifting and unsolid, like the colored ball pit at Chuck E. Cheese. A ball pit of stinking, filthy garbage. Trevor extended his arm to the man. His face was brown and deeply lined. He wore a thin, plaid, button-up shirt with pointed Western-style pocket flourishes. They locked hand-over-forearm and the man climbed out. He was three times Trevor's age, at least, but probably six inches shorter. *Gracias*, he said, and before Trevor could think to ask if he wanted a sandwich, the man hurried off. Trevor wondered how long the man had lived in Canton. How far from home had he traveled to end up falling into a garbage dumpster? Would he have left that place if he'd known? Would Trevor have left Canton if he'd known he'd end up sneaking onto an island off Massachusetts in a desperate attempt to apologize to a girl he hardly knew? He wanted to get to Claudia more than he'd ever wanted anything. He felt helpless against the force of the want. And yes, he wanted to touch her. He wanted her to reach for him. To look into his eyes and say, *I understand. You were trying to keep me safe. I love you, too.* He'd imagined it so many times it felt like it was possible. He walked back down the hill to the bus stop, but the sign said he'd missed the last shuttle of the night. According to the map on his phone it would take two-and-a-half hours to walk to her house.

The wind pressed against him as he moved, head down,

along the sidewalks and bike paths and sandy shoulders connecting the little towns that made up the island. Was this place even real? Would a wave come and wash it all away before sunrise? For one long stretch beside the water, on the island's northeast side, each step forward felt like a feat. When the path turned into trees that blocked the whipping gusts of ocean air, the relief was so profound he momentarily felt as if he were floating.

Her house was surrounded by a low stone wall, partially hidden behind a stand of evergreens that towered over the power lines, their night-black needles swaying thickly overhead. Trevor could see no lights in the house, but the high, bright moon illuminated a gate, and a path. The salt in the air had made the skin on his face stiff. He was thirsty. He climbed the three stone steps to the front door and cupped his hands around the window cut into the top half. If anyone was inside, they were asleep. He tried the handle. Locked. Lightly, he rapped a knuckle against the glass.

"Hello," he said quietly, though he sensed it was to no one but the house itself. He needed to sit down, take a minute, make a plan. He walked back down the steps and turned onto the grass, keeping close to the house as he walked along the front and down toward the water. What he found on the other side was spectacular. Wide tiers of stone patios extending left and right to a swimming pool and farther, down toward the ocean. Outdoor furniture neatly covered, barrel-sized planters, a fire pit, a brick pizza oven. He knew she was rich, but damn. Trevor followed the path to the top patio and the wall of French doors. He looked up at the second level of windows—the bedrooms, he presumed. Was she up there? Was anyone? Was this his Romeo moment? Of course not.

The furniture beneath an overhang was uncovered, so he sat down on the sofa and settled into the understanding that he was going to sleep here tonight. Close to the house so he might hear someone move around inside. Which way was he facing? Maybe he'd open his eyes into the sunrise. Maybe Claudia would bring him a cup of coffee.

His full bladder woke him just after eight a.m. Trevor jogged down to the water and relieved himself before his brain could tell him that getting caught, dick out, in a place like this, would be very bad. He peered in through a side door, seeing a kind of mudroom: slate floors, raincoats on hooks, boots in cubbies. He tried the handle and it opened.

"Claudia?"

The sound of his voice unnerved him. Was he frightened? Desperate? He let the door fall shut behind him, not latching. Something about letting it latch felt too permanent. Like he was making a decision he couldn't run from. *If I don't close the door entirely, maybe I didn't actually come in.* The side room led to a kitchen open to a dining room open to a sprawling living area. It was like the houses on the renovation shows his mom watched. Tables didn't have mail or sunglasses or keys lying on them; there were no sweaters on the backs of chairs. No signs of active life. Vases and books and framed photographs were set purposely, symmetrically, on surfaces. He said Claudia's name again as he walked slowly toward the staircase, which creaked as he climbed it. The landing on the second floor had a leather chair and bookshelves, a telescope beside the window. There was so much space. Down the long hallway, the doors to the bedrooms were open and he peeked into each. Why not? The first had a canopy bed and an old-fashioned porcelain washbasin in the bureau. A silver comb-and-brush set. Framed watercolors of seashells hung over pale yellow-and-white floral wallpaper. Trevor wondered how long it had been since someone slept there. The second bedroom was similarly impersonal: a four-poster bed; black-and-white beach photos framed above the headboard; blue-and-gray striped wallpaper; a blanket folded at the foot of the bed; a book about knots on the little desk at the window.

Claudia's room was different. From the doorway he spotted a series of old-fashioned Polaroids hung by clothespins and strung across the ceiling, dangling like flags. There were probably fifty of them, each with a handwritten date or phrase or symbol penned on it: *July 18; Derby;* ♥♥. In one marked *Spring Break*, Claudia and a girl who looked like her—the sister, maybe?—lay in bikinis on the stark white deck of a boat. Both girls had an arm resting over their eyes. Were they asleep? Were they posing? Looking at her body like that, nearly naked, glistening in the sun, he couldn't help where the blood flowed. It had been more than two weeks since he first saw her in those shorts at the elevators in the dorm, and he hadn't once been able to fall asleep without succumbing to the fantasies about her that swarmed his mind. It felt biologically necessary but morally wrong. And it made him angry; he'd used part of that anger in the Mews. Anger that was confusion. Anger that was disgust. At night, alone in bed, he imagined that even after all she'd been through she could still want him to grab her and kiss her. Girls are funny like that, his brother used to tell him, before prison. Sometimes they want a gentleman, but sometimes they want a predator. You gotta learn to play the game, his brother said. Hold the door and pay for dinner, but back in the bedroom rip off her panties and push her against the wall. Mike told Trevor that the first time he made his high school girlfriend come he had his hands around her throat. Not too hard, he said; just hard enough. Trevor hadn't had the nerve to try it until Whitney and it'd worked. No wonder she hated him.

He adjusted himself and looked around at the rest of the room. An ornate mirror with an iron frame took up much of one wall. Necklaces and scarves and ID badges hung from its corners. Claudia had been backstage at Taylor Swift; she'd been to Coachella and the VMAs multiple times; she'd been to Cannes.

Trevor left Claudia's room and went to a window at the end of the hall, which looked out toward the ocean. The house was still. She wasn't here. No one was. He walked back down the stairs and out the back door to the sofa where he'd slept. He closed his eyes and lifted his head to the sun. Then he called his brother. When Mike didn't pick up, Trevor texted.

it's me—lost my phone and had to get a new number. can you talk??

A moment later, the phone rang.

"Trev?" His brother sounded groggy. "You okay? What time is it there?"

"Sorry." Shit. It was predawn in Ohio.

"What's up?"

Trevor spilled. The video, the Mews, the empty house on the Vineyard.

"Jesus," said his brother. "How long have you been with this girl?"

"We're not together."

"Okay, whatever, hooking up."

"We're not hooking up."

"You've committed two felonies for a girl you're not hooking up with?"

Was that what he'd done?

"You need to get out of that house," said Mike. "Get out of there before somebody finds you."

"I fucked up," said Trevor, his voice breaking. It was all about to come loose.

"Listen to me, Trev. Leave now. Get off that island as fast as you can. If there isn't surveillance of whatever happened with that kid you could get out of this. Unless she said something. You know you can't trust someone you just met, right?"

"I think something bad happened to her."

"I don't know what kind of spell she's got you under," said Mike. "But you need to start thinking about yourself now. You are currently breaking and entering, little brother. You're not fifteen anymore. The law is not on your side. Get the fuck out of there before the police come."

He told his brother he would go but he didn't. One more night. *If she's not here in the morning, I'll go home.* He found a wedge of cheese in the refrigerator and crackers in the pantry, and he ate them standing just inside the French doors, watching the sunset. There was an open bottle of white wine, too, and he finished it, allowing himself fantasies of her approach (*a taxi?*), the explanation (*I just needed some time, she'd say*), their reconciliation (*I understand, she'd say. You were trying to protect me.*). But when the night got dark his mind went back to the hotel room, to Lesley in her black dress, to the bag packed by the door. He didn't really know her, and he had no idea where she might be. Maybe she had never planned to come here. Or maybe when she spoke the idea she'd thought she would, but later changed her mind and didn't tell him. Did that make her selfish? Did it make her cruel? The Claudia he had spent the last two weeks with, he realized, was probably as new to herself as she was to him. What Chad and Jeremy did, what they threatened to continue doing, had to have changed her. It had changed him.

At some point Trevor fell asleep. He dreamed of police cars; red flashing lights, wheels on gravel. He dreamed he was standing in the Mews in the rain but instead of Jeremy coming around the corner it was Mike. *I can't do this*, he thought in the dream. He hit the wooden door on the storybook house beside him with a bat. *Bang bang.* And then he was awake. And someone was at the back door.

TREVOR

The man in the police uniform was coming in through the kitchen.

"Hello," called Trevor. "Hi. I'm a friend of Claudia's."

"Claudia's here?" asked the officer.

"No," he said. "She left. She said it was okay for me to stay."

Why had he lied? He'd made nothing but good decisions after Mike got locked up and nothing but bad since he'd seen that fucking video.

"What's your name, son?"

"Trevor."

"You live on the island?" The officer was probably in his twenties. His hair was white-blond and his name tag read "Cross."

"No," said Trevor.

"Claudia's family is looking for her. They called overnight to say she may have come here. But you're saying she left."

"I meant, she's not here. I was supposed to meet her, but she's not here. I don't know where she is."

"How long have you been here?" asked the officer.

"Since yesterday. I figured maybe she lost her phone and I was actually going to leave last night but I missed the ferry, so I can just take off now . . ."

"Sit down, please," said the officer. "Keep your hands where I can see them."

Trevor sat. Officer Cross pulled out his phone.

"This is Cross," he said to whoever was on the other end. "I'm out here at the Whitehouse place. The kid says he's friends with Claudia." He listened, looking at Trevor, then looking around the room. "No. He seems a little confused about that." More listening. "Right. Okay."

The officer ended the call.

"We're gonna sit tight."

Trevor had to pee. Should he say so?

"How do you know Claudia?" asked the officer.

"We're in the same dorm. Same floor."

"NYU?"

"Yeah."

"You're from the city then?"

"No," he said. "I'm from Ohio."

"Long way from home."

Trevor forced a smile. "Do you mind if I use the bathroom?"

"Not if you don't mind company."

Officer Cross followed Trevor through the dining room to the half bathroom in the hall. Trevor stood at the door as the officer checked the room, maybe noting that the window was too small for a human being to climb through.

"Make it quick," he said.

"Yes, sir."

Trevor peed and flushed and replaced the seat, turned on the water, looked in the mirror above the sink. *You can do this*, he told himself. As he dried his hands he heard the sound of wheels on gravel. Has that been the sound in his dream? He looked out the window and saw a pickup. A white-haired man got out of the passenger seat and walked toward the back of the house.

"Let's get moving," said Officer Cross.

In the living room he instructed Trevor to sit back down on the sofa and met the white-haired man at the patio door. Trevor strained to hear what the men were saying, but couldn't make out words. After what felt like an hour but was probably just a few minutes, Officer Cross and the white-haired man came back into the living room.

"I'm going to need you to come with me," said the officer.

The jail on the island was housed inside a small building with white wood siding and green shutters. It could have been any of the houses he'd seen on the drive from Claudia's, except for the bars on the windows, the perfunctory landscaping, and the aluminum handicapped ramp. Trevor was taken to an empty holding cell on the second floor, with wooden benches lining the walls. They took his phone, so he could measure the passing time only by the light and the growing discomfort in his empty stomach. He was preparing his story. It was mostly true. She'd told him he could come. She'd given him the address. Why had he said she was there? He was going to have to walk that back and that was going to make him look suspicious. But of course he would look suspicious. He *was* suspicious. He was a desperate boy with blood on his hands. And his brother was right: He wasn't even a boy anymore. At least in the eyes of the law, he was a man.

Eventually Officer Cross and a woman with a gun clipped to her belt and a folder under her arm came to the cell and escorted him through a series of locked doors, down a flight of stairs, and into a room with floor-to-ceiling bookshelves along three walls and a table so massive and old it looked like it might have been used to sign the Constitution. The woman introduced herself as Lieutenant Lucinda Braga. She folded her hands on the table, leaned forward, and looked Trevor directly in the eye.

"Claudia's family is on their way from Manhattan," she told him. "They haven't seen or heard from her in nearly two weeks."

She paused and watched his reaction.

"Did you know that?"

"That Claudia hadn't seen them? Yeah. She was sort of avoiding them. Actually she thought they were avoiding her."

"Well, they're extremely concerned," Lt. Braga said gravely. "If you tell me where she is I think we can make all this go away."

"I don't know where she is," said Trevor.

She let him sit with that.

"I don't," he said.

"When was the last time you saw her?"

"On Saturday. In Manhattan."

"You told Officer Cross she was at the house but that she left."

"I misspoke. I meant she told me I could come visit. She told me she was coming here."

"You misspoke."

"I was nervous. I'm sorry."

Lt. Braga stared at him, assessing his truthfulness, he guessed.

"I'm really sorry," he said again.

"What are you sorry about?"

"About . . . misspeaking."

"Claudia's family has a lot of questions. And you should think very hard about whether you want to "misspeak" again. You can cooperate; you can tell the truth; or you can end up like your brother."

"What?" he managed to croak.

"We might be a small town, but we know how to background stalkers."

"You think I'm a—"

"Let me fill you in what I know. I know you've been spending a lot of time with Claudia, but her family hasn't seen her in weeks. And none of them had ever heard of you before yesterday. I also know you have a juvenile record in Ohio." She paused to let that sink in, and it did. He should have known nothing is really "sealed" these days. Nothing done can be undone. "Claudia's family suspects she is in danger. And as you may have gathered when you were trespassing in their home, they are the kind of people whose suspicions get humored. So we have to be on our game here. Leave no stone unturned. Which is why I'm going to ask you again: Where is Claudia?"

"I really don't know," he said. "I thought she was going to be here. She told me she was going to be here."

"Did you hurt her?"

"No!" He said it too loudly. He was scared, but to the cops he probably looked hostile. Possibly dangerous. Mike had done the same thing. His brother's lawyer said that part of the reason the DA wouldn't let Mike off without prison time was because he thought his brother had "violent tendencies" after the cops told him Mike had kicked a chair in the interrogation room. A fucking chair. Trevor looked at the table. He put his hands flat in front of him, and took a deep breath.

"No," he said. "I would never hurt Claudia."

"Were you in love with her?"

"What? No." Was that a lie?

"It's okay if you were. Love's not a crime."

Trevor didn't answer. He thought of that line in *Hamilton* that Boyd was always singing: *Talk less, smile more.*

"If something happened, an accident, maybe?" continued Lt. Braga. "It's in your interest to tell us. Because if we find a body . . ."

"A body? She's dead?"

"You tell me."

"You're the one talking about bodies. Is there something you're not telling me?" That was a stupid question. There were probably fifty things they weren't telling him. It was practically their job not to tell him things. This was a test and he was failing.

"Calm down," said Lt. Braga. "Maybe something happened, some sort of accident, and you feel responsible. Maybe you were doing drugs together. Do you know how many ODs we get on this island every month? Maybe you panicked."

Was Claudia actually lying on a slab somewhere? Or was she just making shit up? Trevor knew he hadn't hurt Claudia, but there were several people whose lives would be more comfortable if she were gone. And he was not going to take the fall for them.

"I don't want to answer any more questions without a lawyer," he said.

Lt. Braga and Officer Cross looked at each other, eyebrows raised, a little performance of surprise.

"All right" said Lt. Braga, standing up. "We do things by the book here. I don't suppose you have anyone on retainer?"

"What?"

Lt. Braga smirked. "Will you be needing a public defender?"

"Yes," He couldn't believe he was here again. "Can I call someone?"

"Soon."

Lt. Braga left and Officer Cross told him to stand up.

They left the Constitution room and just before they reached the stairs, they passed a door with a window that looked onto what appeared to be an entry hall. Standing in the hall, talking to another man in a uniform, was Ridley Drake. Trevor stopped walking.

"Keep walking, please."

"What is he doing here?" The understanding shook his stomach. His legs went hot. Claudia had come to the island, and Ridley had followed her, and . . . What? Trevor banged on the window.

"What did you do to her?"

Ridley turned but Trevor didn't get to see his expression because Officer Cross pushed him forward.

"Where is Claudia?" Trevor shouted. He looked at Officer Cross, trying to regain his composure. He needed the officer to listen. He needed the officer to believe him.

"Please," said Trevor, struggling for a breath.

Officer Cross grabbed his right wrist and twisted it back, then his left. It seemed like one motion. Suddenly he was in handcuffs.

"Move!" said the officer.

"Ask him about Claudia!" screamed Trevor. "Ask him!"

EDIE

They'd been scheduled to take off from JFK at ten a.m. but winds and then a mechanical problem and then a shift change meant the family spent seven hours in the airport trying to remain calm. Edie and Nathan took turns walking Lydia up and down the terminal, while Gabe and Michelle fell into their phones, getting sporadic updates from the Vineyard: An officer was at the house; Trevor was in custody; no sign of Claudia.

Lt. Lucinda Braga and Dave Wilcox were waiting at the airport. Dave drove the family home with the lieutenant following and when they pulled up, the chief of police was standing in the driveway with two uniformed officers. What was he going to tell them? Edie began shaking. *Please, God*, she thought, looking down at Lydia. *Please.*

Edie strapped the baby to her chest and followed her

parents inside while Nathan and Dave unloaded the car. The bottle of wine and the plate and napkin and handful of utensils Trevor had used were still on the coffee table. Chief Frank Kittery, a tall, thick-necked man with a moustache and a military haircut, guided the family to the dining room table. Edie remained standing, swaying and lightly bouncing, trying to keep Lydia quiet. The chief explained that Trevor had been cooperative at first but that his story was inconsistent, that he had a juvenile record, and that he'd resisted an officer at the jail facility.

"He says he doesn't know where Claudia is," said Lt. Braga.

"Do you believe him?" asked Gabe.

"I do, actually," said Lt. Braga. "But I could be wrong. We're not done with him. Especially now that he's made an accusation against Ridley Drake."

The chief eyed Michelle. Apparently he read the *Post*, too.

"What sort of accusation?" asked Edie.

"He claims Mr. Drake's son recorded a sexual encounter with Claudia," said the chief. "He also claims that Mr. Drake stole his phone, which he says has a copy of the encounter on it."

"He called it an encounter?" asked Edie.

"What's important is—"

"What's important," said Michelle, "is that Chad Drake filmed himself raping my daughter."

Without even a glance between them, Gabe took the iPhone from his pocket and handed it to Michelle, who handed it to the chief. Edie considered leaving the room but it occurred to her that she was probably going to have to deal with this video for a long time, and she'd better start getting used to it. She'd better start getting strong. Claudia had to endure it; the least she could do was bear to watch it. She put her hands over Lydia's ears.

Fifty-eight seconds felt like an hour.

The chief spoke first. "I'm not sure what I'm looking at here."

Asshole, Edie thought. He probably got off on porn like that every night. He could take the video as evidence and get off on it at home. He could pass it to a friend. Or ten. That's what Claudia was running from, Edie realized. And the truth was that she'd never be able to run far enough.

"Ridley knows," said Michelle "Ask him."

"Did you know that Mr. Drake was here the day before yesterday?" asked Lt. Braga.

The chief glared at his subordinate. "Lieutenant," he said.

"Here? At this house?" asked Michelle.

Lt. Braga nodded; the chief appeared annoyed.

"I did not know. What was he doing?"

"After we took the boy from Ohio into custody we asked your neighbors for any footage from security cameras. The people just across from you captured a white Tesla driving up and the driver getting out early yesterday. It was Mr. Drake."

"Lieutenant," said the captain, "Mr. Drake explained that."

"Oh, really," said Gabe. "How did he explain it?"

The captain hesitated.

"Our daughter is *missing*, Chief Kittery," said Michelle. "How did Ridley Drake explain being at our home?"

"He said he thought you were here," said Lt. Braga. "But when no one answered, he left."

"He said he thought *I* was here?" asked Michelle.

"Yes."

"That's bullshit. He had zero reason to think that."

"Look," said the chief. "I don't really want to get into the middle of what is clearly a complicated situation . . ."

"You need to ask Ridley Drake about my daughter," said Michelle. "I realize that most of your so-called work here consists of golfing and cocktails but you are *supposed* to be a police officer. You have a witness in your custody who says that Ridley Drake stole his phone—a phone that had evidence of a crime on it. You now have a copy of that evidence—of Ridley's son *committing a crime* against my daughter. My daughter who hasn't been at school, hasn't communicated with her friends or family, and hasn't been on social media in almost two weeks. We believe she is in danger. She was seen with a ticket to Woods Hole last weekend and the boy you have in custody says she was planning to come to the island. Do your job and look for her."

"The airport has no record of her flying in," offered Lt. Braga. "We have officers looking at footage from the ferry. If she was here, we'll find out."

"But until then," said the chief, "I'm sure you understand that I can't just force citizens to answer questions based on speculation."

"Nobody's asking you to force anyone," said Nathan.

"They're asking you to try. If you actually wanted to find Claudia you'd try. Unless you're afraid, for some reason."

"Afraid?"

Nathan shrugged his shoulders. "Ridley Drake is a big shit, right? 'Prominent lawyer.'"

"He's got something on everybody," said Edie. It was something he'd told her that summer: Information is just as valuable as money. More, sometimes. You want to know which judge has a secret kid; which one is a pothead; which ADA has a daughter with a shoplifting issue. Which one is having an affair with a hot teenager. He'd laughed. And she'd laughed, too. She'd been flattered. *An affair.* "What's he got on you?"

"I think we're done here," said the chief. "I understand you're concerned . . ."

"You're a piece of shit," spat Michelle.

The chief spoke through his teeth. "If I could be sure that this video isn't doctored in some way, or if I had reason to think that it wasn't simply depicting what most college students do on a Friday night, or if I could prove it was filmed in my jurisdiction, maybe I would have probable cause to bring Chad in. Not his father. It doesn't work like that."

"We're not asking you to bring him in," said Gabe. "We're asking you to have a conversation with him."

"I'm sorry," said the chief, "I recognize that you're not used to being told no. But I won't be pressured. Not by anyone."

The chief signaled to the uniformed officers. "Lt. Braga," he said. She stood up but lingered a moment after he'd gone.

"We'll get back to you if we find anything on the ferry cameras."

"Thank you," said Edie.

Lt. Braga looked at Michelle. "Drake's still on the island as far as I know," she said, handing Edie's mother a business card. "Reach out if you need anything."

When the lieutenant left, Edie realized they hadn't gotten half the information they needed. What was happening to Trevor? What else did he have to say? Could they talk to him? She looked to her mother to say they should call Lt. Braga back but Michelle already had the phone to her ear.

"You're on the Vineyard?" she asked. She was talking to Ridley. "Yes . . . Where is Claudia? . . . When was the last time you saw him? . . . I'm coming over." She ended the call and looked at her family. "We're going to Ridley's."

Ridley Drake's house was about a mile outside Edgartown proper, on the road to Katama Beach. Matching stacked stone pillars marked the driveway, and a long slope of grass, acres of grass, sloped toward the water and the house, sprawling along the shore. Edie could see a few rooms illuminated inside and a motion light clicked on as they approached, revealing glass walls and tiers of bluestone patios, decks, an infinity pool. The driveway was paved in a herringbone pattern; three garage doors, all closed. Nathan was going to stay outside with Lydia. She'd sleep in the car seat or he'd walk her until they came out.

"Just start screaming if you need me," he told her.

Edie kissed her husband and her daughter, and as she followed her mom and dad up the stairs to Ridley's front door, she pulled out her phone and pressed the red button on the voice record app. Whatever he said would be used against him.

When he opened the door and saw them all standing there, Edie thought she saw Ridley flinch. Had he just expected Michelle?

"I told you I don't know where she is," said Ridley.

Michelle walked in past him. How many times had her mom been inside this house? It was being renovated the summer he and Edie had been together and once they had sex in a room with no walls or roof. Just the wooden framing and the drop cloths and the stars above. It was the only time he'd brought her here; in the dark.

"I wish I knew," he said. "Believe me. I've been doing everything I can to contain this.

"*Contain* this?" said Michelle, glowing with rage. "You mean keep Claudia from filing rape charges against your son?"

Ridley was sweating. He was angry, too, but he didn't take the bait. Gabe shut the door.

"What were you doing at our house?" asked Michelle. "Was she there?"

"If she was she didn't answer the door."

"What were you going to do if she did?"

"I was going to talk some sense into her, Michelle!" The volume of his voice startled Edie. The words seemed to detonate inside the room, the blasting syllables knocked around the walls and bounced off the windows. No one responded. Ridley took a deep breath through his teeth, disdain souring his face.

"I was going to make sure she understood her choices," he

said, now studiously somber. "I was going to encourage her to talk to you. And to get some help."

"And what would you say her choices are?" asked Michelle.

"I wanted her to know how it works in the real world. I wanted her to know what happens *after* she shows that video to the police. It's not going to be, oh, poor you, sweet victim, those bad boys go to jail. Not by a long shot. All that video does is open her up to questions. How did you get so drunk that night, Claudia? Why so many shots? Where did you get that fake ID? Why did you go up to his room? Why did you post that selfie? And what about this post from last month, the one with all the cleavage? And what about that TV show? You know, Claudia, it seems like maybe you have a pattern of getting drunk and doing things you don't remember. Would you call yourself an alcoholic?"

Edie watched Ridley's performance and bile started to rise in her throat. He was the worst of everything and she'd let him strangle her spirit for almost two years. He was always going to be there, his dismissal, the degradation, the fetus she'd had to have removed from her body because of him. But as she watched him lecture them all, she realized that she didn't have to hate the eighteen-year-old who let him into her life anymore. Ridley was like the wind: If he wanted in, he was getting in, whether the door was open or not.

"I wanted to tell your sister," he continued, now looking

directly at Edie, "that even if she answers all these questions to their satisfaction, the DA is never going to take her case to trial because she will be under indictment for felony assault of my son. She will be the definition of an unreliable witness."

"What are you talking about?" asked Gabe.

"Your daughter has serious problems, Michelle. No wonder she disappeared."

"She disappeared because of what Chad did to her!" screamed Edie. "He's just like you. He thinks he can do anything. But he can't. You can't scare us. We've got the video and we're going to the police. You think Claudia can't stand up to some *questions*? Claudia is a fucking hero."

She had everyone's attention now. Her body felt better than it had in weeks. The strength she needed *finally* kicking in.

"Did you steal that kid's phone?" Edie asked him.

"Eden," said Ridley. He stepped forward and put his hand on her arm, a light, intimate touch. "You need to calm down, honey."

Michelle grabbed Edie's hand and pulled her close.

"Back up, motherfucker." Michelle's eyes were wide, nostrils flaring: her face ugly with the horror of what she suddenly suspected. *This is what Ridley did,* Edie thought. *He made the people around him ugly.*

"Trevor told the cops you stole his phone," Edie said again. "Did you?"

"I offered him a lot of money and he wouldn't take it. That

kid is in way over his head, okay? He's lucky we didn't press charges on him after he attacked Chad, in broad daylight."

"I wonder why?" said Gabe.

Ridley turned to Edie's dad. "He speaks."

He'd barely gotten the words out when Gabe whacked him across the face with a coffee table book.

"What the fuck!" shouted Ridley, stumbling sideways. His leg caught the corner of a side table and he crashed to the ground, knocking over a vase full of wildflowers that shattered when it hit. An explosion of glass and water.

"Do you know where Claudia is?" Gabe asked, now standing over him, struggling to keep his voice steady. Edie had seen her father this angry only once before, a decade ago, when he kicked in a door the night he learned his dad had died in a car accident.

Ridley tried to get to his feet but Gabe kicked him in the stomach.

"No!" shouted Ridley. "I don't know where she is! All I know is she sliced my son with a box cutter in a motel room last weekend. If I were her I'd go to Mexico. Or jump off a fucking bridge."

Silence dropped over the room. Edie looked at Ridley's bleeding, aggrieved face and thought: *we will destroy you.*

"We'd better not find out you're lying," said Michelle.

Edie took her mom's hand and tugged her toward the door. Gabe followed. They were done here.

No one spoke on the way home. Back in the house, Nathan walked Lydia upstairs and Edie's parents asked her to stay down on the first floor.

"Your father shared what you told him," whispered Michelle. "Can I . . ." Her mother stepped forward, her face red and wet and crumpled, crying openly, and wrapped her arms around Edie. "I'm so sorry, baby. I . . ."

"It's okay, Mom," said Edie, closing her eyes and allowing herself to fall into the comfort, the closure, of the embrace. "I'm okay. Let's just find Claudia."

CLAUDIA

The guy who attacked her at TGI Fridays heard the bartender say her ticket was for Woods Hole, so she couldn't go to the Vineyard. As Claudia rushed through the Port Authority to the escalator at the corner of Forty-First Street, her teeth were chattering. Her body screamed, *Go!* She had no more fight in her, only flight. She had to get off the island.

The last train to Poughkeepsie left in an hour. She was pretty sure Edie and Nathan kept a key under the mat. She bought a quarter bottle of wine and a bag of popcorn at a bodega around the corner from Grand Central and got a seat by the window on the 11:59 leaving from Track 71.

As the train pulled above ground in Harlem, the hot buzz of adrenaline that had been roaring through her body since she put the blade to Chad's face began its work on her brain.

Were they all in on it? Ridley had to have sent the guy at the bar. Did Trevor tell him where she'd be? For all she knew Ridley and Chad had given Trevor money to bump into her at the dorm. Ridley could have even told her mom about the video. Maybe that's why Edie had been so cold. Maybe they were disgusted. Maybe they really were worried about her germs.

Claudia looked at her reflection in the scratched plastic window. She watched herself drink wine from the bottle. She reached into her bag and found the PReP pills she was supposed to take. *Look at Claudia Castro,* she thought. *Chasing her HIV meds with wine. Claudia Castro is a drama queen. Claudia Castro is a slut. Did Claudia Castro know the guy at the pool party had a girlfriend? Did she care? Is Claudia Castro crazy?*

There were two cabs idling in the roundabout outside the Poughkeepsie station. She gave the driver her sister's address, and when he started the car her bag fell forward, spilling the contents onto the floor of the back seat. The bottle of wine, the box cutter in the plastic bag,

"Big night in the city?" asked the driver. She could see him looking at her from the rearview mirror, a tired smile on his face. Would he believe her if she told the truth? Would anyone?

The house that her sister and Nathan had been living in since they graduated was near the end of a residential street in a hilly neighborhood just off Vassar's campus. It had a screened-in front porch and an old door knocker shaped like a fish and chipping blue-painted shutters. Claudia paid the cabbie and shouldered her bag, watching as he drove off. There was a light on two houses away but every other window on the street was dark. Above, clouds drifted by, swiping lazily across the sky.

The key was where she thought it would be, and inside the only sound was the *tick tick* of a waving Chinese good luck cat on the windowsill. The last time she'd been here she and Edie had gotten in an argument. Edie was just starting to show and Claudia asked if she was having second thoughts.

"About what?" asked her sister, though she knew exactly what Claudia meant.

"About turning your life into a Bruce Springsteen song."

Claudia had laughed at what she thought was a mostly harmless dig but the words hit Edie in the heart. Of course Edie was having second thoughts. Who wouldn't? Nobody pretended the pregnancy was planned. It was a make-the-best-of-a-bad-situation situation. Edie told her she was being mean and Claudia protested and then Edie said fine, not mean, just thoughtless. Edie was right. She had been thoughtless. Just like she'd been when she got too drunk with Chad Drake. What did she expect?

There was a glass overturned in the drying rack. Claudia filled it with water and took her bag into the living room. Mismatched picture frames on the mantel above a fireplace that didn't work; a pile of board games in the corner; a record player on the bar cart. Her sister was happy here. It was the kind of home where a "normal" family might live: a family where Mom and Dad go to work and then come home for dinner and stay. Not many people Claudia and Edie grew up with had families like that. Families where parents at least pretended that home and kids were as interesting as the world outside. Claudia's childhood home had been a way station for the four of them; a shared space but never a shared spirit. This house had Edie and Nathan braided together inside. It almost seemed like magic: her sister had created a happy family.

Standing there, Claudia thought: *I'll never have that.* She knew that she could only begin to imagine all the ways the last two weeks would knock her around. Every night for the rest of her life she was going to close her eyes and get it from one side or the other: what they did and what she did. One side would press and the other side would press and eventually her brain would break. Who wants to be a family with that girl? That girl shouldn't procreate. That girl will only sow misery.

In the morning she went to the kitchen and from the window above the sink Claudia could see the long bridge over the Hudson River. According to Google Maps, she could walk there in less than an hour.

Claudia felt like she was watching herself, like in the window on the train. She walked toward the leafy, stone-walled campus; down Main, the drag that held the pizza shop and the wine shop and the coffee shop and the diner and the bookstore and the laundromat; and farther, the barber shop and bodega and cell phone store. She turned toward the river and the part of town the students rarely ventured through. It was early and the sidewalks were mostly empty. She walked past gas stations and boarded-up town houses, municipal buildings and a public park. Hadn't there been a serial killer who lived nearby? Yes; Claudia remembered that one of Edie's friends did an art project about the victims for her senior thesis. That word again.

Where the pathway toward the bridge turned into the walkway across it, Claudia encountered a green-and-blue metal sign: LIFE IS WORTH LIVING. And a phone number.

She walked out to the middle and put her face into the wind. Below, the water was mesmerizing; churning, running eventually to the harbor in the city, to the foot of Liberty Island, to the ocean, to Europe. Those first nights alone in the hotel Claudia had made the mistake of Googling. She read about a girl in Canada who gassed herself in the family garage after some boys sent around a video of her. And another in the Midwest who jumped off the top of an abandoned factory. Claudia held onto the railing and closed her eyes, tilting her face to the sun. When she felt the warmth against her cheeks she knew she wouldn't do it. Chad Drake was not going to take anything else from her. She was hard now, she was careening; maybe she always would be. But she was not going to give up sunny days on the water. She was not going to let him steal that, too.

She started walking back toward town, past the LIFE IS WORTH LIVING sign. *What did the rest of the girls do?* she wondered. Where were the articles about the girls who lived with it? If life was worth living after this, where could she find out how?

Claudia walked from noon to sundown all the next four days. Over the bridge to New Paltz and back; down to the old cemetery;

through parks along the water. She brought home frozen dinners and ate a few bites. She closed every shade and turned on every lamp and checked the locks on every door and window. Her old phone was off but the new one was always with her, available to dial 911 if Ridley's SUV came rolling up. At night she stared at the television, or the front door. Only when the gray light of a sunrise began to creep into the house did she retreat to the spare bedroom and fall into a black, dreamless sleep.

On the fifth afternoon there was a woman on the front steps when she came outside for her walk.

"Claudia?" The woman was white, fifties maybe, wearing a flowered dress and pantyhose and carrying a heavy key ring. "Are you Edie's sister?"

It was Nathan's mom. She'd driven by the night before and seen the lights, she said. When she called her son to ask if someone was staying at the house she found out they were frantically searching for Claudia.

"They'll be so glad to know you're okay!"

Claudia considered her choices. In theory, she could keep moving. She could go anywhere. But she was far too tired. Nathan's mom left and Claudia sat waiting in her sister's living room. Would they forgive her? They might not. Maybe what she'd done was unforgivable. But maybe they'd still take care of her.

An Uber brought her parents and her sister and her brother-in-law and her niece to the house a few hours later. Edie jumped from the car and ran toward her. No one had touched her for more than a moment since the night she still couldn't remember, and when Edie pressed her chest into

Claudia, she expected to stiffen, but her sister's arms around her felt like nourishment. As if Edie's body were a door closing against the draft Chad and Jeremy had left blowing cold inside. Maybe she could finally get warm.

On the drive back to Manhattan Gabe called the police in Edgartown and told them the family didn't wish to press trespassing charges against Trevor. Claudia got on the phone with Lt. Braga.

"It was a misunderstanding," she said. "I told him he could stay there."

Lydia was quiet through most of the car ride but awoke screaming as they crossed the George Washington Bridge.

"Is she hungry?" Claudia asked, looking back. Edie and Nathan were sitting on either side of Lydia in her car seat in the SUV's third row. Claudia and her parents took up the seat in the car's middle. Mom and dad and daughter. Mom and dad and daughter. For the past hour she'd been watching her niece sleep in the window's reflection. She couldn't stop staring. What horrible things awaited this little girl? What people would cut her low? What people would fail her? What moments would define her? What mistakes would she carry forever? Did she have any control at all? Did anyone?

In the living room Edie plopped down, unhooked her tank top, and wrestled the wailing child across her chest.

"Smell that?" asked Michelle, setting her purse on the breakfront. "I think she needs to be changed."

"There's wipes right here," said Gabe.

Claudia watched her family mobilize around Edie and the baby. When was the last time they were even together in the house? When Lydia finally quieted there was silence, and they all turned toward her.

"Are you hungry?" asked her dad.

"No."

"Tired?"

Claudia nodded.

"What can we do?" asked her mom, stepping toward her.

"I don't know," said Claudia.

"Get some sleep," said her dad. "We're not going anywhere."

Upstairs she took pajamas from her bureau, changed her clothes, and went into the bathroom she and Edie had shared for the past decade. It was just as Claudia had left it the last time she was here, a few days before spring break started. Her face wash and her lotions and her toothbrush evenly spaced on the marble countertop; dried eucalyptus in the ceramic vase she'd made in elementary school; thick gray towels, tastefully mismatched glass pulls on all the drawers; every stray hair or stain wiped away by Valeria, the woman whose job it was to make every surface in their house look beautiful all the time. But nobody could wipe away what had changed on the face she saw in the mirror. Her eye and lip were almost completely healed, just the faintest blue shadow remained on her eyelid, but what she saw when she met her own eyes was someone who had never been in this house before. A stranger to everyone but herself.

TREVOR

Claudia's family had come and gone, he was told.

"She's been hiding out in one of their other houses," said Officer Cross when he brought Trevor a tray for dinner.

"She's okay?" he asked.

Cross shrugged. "Apparently."

The relief was delicious: He hadn't gotten her killed. He hadn't driven her to suicide. It was all going to be over soon. Claudia would explain that they'd had a plan to meet at her house and the cops would let him go and he'd be back at the dorm by tomorrow.

Trevor spent that night in the cell, but instead of being released, in the morning he was escorted into a van and to the courthouse down the road. In a little room in the basement he met with Amy Monroe, a lawyer appointed to represent him in the arraignment. She had sweat stains on her blouse and carried a Citgo travel mug so big it probably held an entire pot of coffee.

"How do you want to plead?" she asked.

"Hasn't anyone talked to Claudia?"

"Who?"

"Claudia Castro?"

"You're going to have to give me more than that."

"It's her house. I was in her house but she told me I could be there. We're friends. Can someone call her?"

"You were arrested at the Whitehouse property."

Trevor stared at her. "She lives there. I mean, I think . . ."

"Oh right," said Amy, flipping pages in the file with his name on it. "Her mom is a Whitehouse. Claudia Castro. So, not guilty? You're friends with her? She said you could stay?"

"Yes."

"What about the resisting charge?"

"I wasn't resisting."

"Not guilty?"

"Can you call her? She should know I'm here."

"What's her number?"

Did anyone know anyone's number? "It's in my phone."

"I'll see what I can do. Do you know anyone on the island?"

"Besides Claudia?"

"Besides Claudia."

"No."

"Can someone post bail if you get it?"

"I don't know. How much?"

"Probably two to five thousand."

He was going to crush his parents. "Maybe."

Amy left, and about thirty minutes later a guard came in.

"Trevor Barber, you're up." The guard was carrying handcuffs. He was going to be walked into a courtroom in handcuffs. Where *the fuck* was Claudia?

The guard walked him up a stairwell and through a door in the back of the courtroom. Amy Monroe was at the defense table, tapping away at her phone. When she looked up, she stood.

"Your honor," she said. "I respectfully ask that the bailiff uncuff my client. It's completely unnecessary and frankly, prejudicial."

Trevor stopped. Should he keep walking?

"Keep moving," said the bailiff, motioning to the seat next to Amy.

"Everyone sit down," said the judge. He was entirely bald, with a long, thin face and wire-rimmed glasses perched on the tip of his nose. "Mr. Farmington? Did you request this defendant be handcuffed?"

"I did not, your honor," said the man at the prosecuting table. Trevor could only see his profile. His stomach strained against his belt, and something—a tissue, maybe—poked out of his pants pocket.

"Bailiff please uncuff the defendant," said the judge. "Mr. Farmington, please state the case against this defendant."

"The people allege, your honor, that two days ago defendant Trevor Barber broke into a private home in Edgartown. The home belongs to Michelle Whitehouse and Gabriel Castro. When confronted by police, Mr. Barber lied, and later resisted arrest. Mr. Barber has no connection to Dukes

County. He is a student at New York University and his family lives in Canton, Ohio. This morning we received a call from the New York City Police Department whose detectives would like to question Mr. Barber about an assault in Manhattan. Given that, I think it would be prudent to hold the defendant without bail."

"Is the defendant a suspect in this Manhattan assault?" asked the judge.

"Not that I'm aware of, your honor." The prosecutor took the white cloth from his pocket and wiped his nose with it.

"That's not a particularly helpful answer, counsel. Did the detectives say he was a suspect?"

"I'm sorry, your honor. No, they did not go into specifics."

"Yes or no, please."

"No." The prosecutor sneezed into his tissue. "Excuse me, your honor. I've got a bit of a cold. They did not say he was considered a suspect."

"Thank you," said the judge. Trevor's body was nearly frozen with fear but he could see that while the prosecutor was trying to make him look like a menace, the judge wasn't necessarily buying it. Might he get lucky? "Is the defendant accused of doing any damage at the home he allegedly broke into?"

"Not that we know of."

"You don't know what he's been accused of?"

"I'm sorry, your honor. I meant that Edgartown police are currently looking into . . ." The prosecutor sneezed again, and this time he didn't get his tissue up in time. "Excuse me, your honor."

"Let's move this along, shall we?" said the judge. "Mr. Farmington, I do not appreciate you bringing your virus into my courtroom. After this case, please arrange to have one of your associates take your place until you are well." Before the prosecutor could respond, the judge turned to Trevor's table. "How does your client plead, Ms. Monroe."

"Not guilty on both counts, your honor," she said, standing.

"Mr. Barber?"

Was he supposed to speak now? To stand? Amy put her hand on his shoulder indicating he was.

"Yes," he said, getting up. "Not guilty."

Should he sit down?

"You may sit down," said the judge. "I suppose you think I should set bail, counselor?"

"I absolutely do, your honor. As I'm sure you know I've just been handed this case but my client assures me this is a big misunderstanding."

"How so?"

"My client says that Ms. Castro is a friend from school and they'd made plans to meet at the house."

"And what does Ms. Castro say?"

"I haven't had a chance to speak to her yet," said Amy. "Like I said . . ."

"I know, you just got the case." The judge turned to the prosecutor. "Mr. Farmington, has anyone from your office talked with Ms. Castro or her family?"

The prosecutor did not answer immediately. Trevor turned his head to see what was causing the delay and saw that the prosecutor was holding his tissue over his nose and mouth and whispering with a woman in the first row of benches behind him.

"Mr. Farmington," said the judge.

"I'm sorry, your honor. Yes, we *have* had a message from the family. It came in overnight."

"And?"

"I'm sorry, it appears to have been missing from my file." He sneezed again. "Excuse me. But my clerk is telling me that Ms. Castro called and confirmed she had told Mr. Barber he could stay."

"Well, that seems like pretty important information, Mr. Farmington. Let's see if I can do your job for you. Is the family here now, on the island?"

Trevor turned toward the back door. Was she going to walk in? What would he do if she walked in?

"They are not, your honor," said the prosecutor. "But I should also point out that the defendant is charged with resisting arrest. As you know, we take the safety of our law enforcement personnel seriously in Dukes County, and until I am able to speak with the officer *and* the Whitehouse family I'd like to make sure this man doesn't get on the ferry and deprive our citizens of justice served."

"Bail is set at two thousand dollars," said the judge. He banged his gavel.

The bailiff took Trevor by the arm.

"I'd like a moment to confer with my client, please," said Amy.

"Not on my time," said the bailiff. "You know where he'll be."

"Call somebody for that bail," said Amy as he walked away. "I'll talk to the family."

Trevor sat alone in the basement of the courthouse for hours, his mind wobbling among the problems in front of him. What was he going to tell the NYPD? Had someone actually seen him in the Mews? Trevor hadn't even considered the possibility that there were security cameras in the alley. He was in so far over his head. Was he caught on tape? Was there a screenshot of his face beneath that purple cap being emailed to cops all over the city? He thought of that image and then he thought of his parents seeing it. Seeing him in the act. Seeing how badly their boy had fucked up, right there in black and white. They would shoulder the responsibility again; search themselves for ways they'd failed. They'd spend the rest of their lives searching.

Could he ask Boyd for the bail? Boyd probably had $2,000 available. But would he have to come to the island and actually post the money in person? That was a big ask. Trevor's parents had to physically retrieve him from the jail in Canton, but he'd been underage then. Probably there was some way to pay online now. Pastor Evan would come, but Trevor couldn't ask the church for money. Claudia could afford it. Would she say yes if he asked?

At the end of the day, Trevor and a woman his mom's age were driven back to the jail building. Trevor wondered what the woman had done to end up there and what she was guessing about him.

The officer on duty told Trevor to wait while he took the woman upstairs. When he returned, he uncuffed Trevor and handed him a file.

"Your bail has been paid," he said. "Take this. You're due back in court May eleventh."

"Who paid it?"

"Your lawyer. He's waiting outside."

Ridley wasn't in the backseat of an SUV this time, but standing casually beside a white Tesla.

"Ready to go home?" he asked. "We can still catch the ferry. You'll be at the dorm by midnight, latest."

"I'm not getting in your car."

"Oh, come on, I'm not going to *hurt* you. They know I paid your bail. I'm waving, look, I'm waving at the surveillance camera. Hello! Yes, I'm taking this young man to Manhattan. If anything happens to him, I did it." He started walking toward the driver's side. "Satisfied? Let's go. I don't want to miss the ferry."

Trevor got in. They rode in silence to the harbor. Ridley pulled the car into the hull of the ship and parked behind an Audi.

"I'm going to get a drink. You want a drink?"

"No."

"Fine," said Ridley, shutting his door. "Be back here when we dock."

Trevor waited a few minutes for Ridley to get in front of him, then took the stairs three flights up to the top deck and watched the lights of the island fade away. The air was cool and the breeze picked up as they moved. *I'm on the ocean*, he thought. *Am I on the ocean?* He took a picture of the life preserver at the prow that read MARTHA'S VINEYARD in red letters. He had a feeling he'd never be back.

Trevor returned to the Tesla as the boat backed toward shore. Ridley was already in the driver's seat.

"Do you want to listen to something?" he asked. "It's a good four hours to the Village. Which podcasts do you like?"

"I don't really have time for podcasts these days," said Trevor.

"They're working you hard at school? Good, that's good. That's what you're there for, right? Chad hasn't complained but to be honest, we're not that close. His mom pretty much raised him. How about music? What's your favorite band?"

"I don't have one."

"Okay. What about decades? Forget it, we'll do eighties. You're okay with eighties? Fine."

At some point, after the sky went dark and the red and yellow lights on the road started to sting his eyes, Trevor let himself nod off. A dream came immediately: He was knocking on Claudia's dorm-room door. He was drunk, head spinning, words tumbling out like rocks from a bag. The door opened; when he saw his mom and dad the words turned to sounds. He was grunting and spitting like an animal, kneeling on the floor. And then, from behind him, a hand on his shoulder and her voice: "Trevor, it'll be all right. I promise."

He awoke with a gasp. Ridley had turned down the radio.

"I was going to let you sleep."

Trevor straightened up, looked out the window.

"Mohegan Sun's coming up. You want to stop off? Play some games? Get a steak?"

Was he serious?

"I'm good," said Trevor.

"Cool. Just trying to be friendly. Figured you might want to blow off some steam."

"In a casino?"

"Okay, that's not your thing."

Ridley dropped the subject and turned the music up.

"Do you think I've forgotten that you robbed me?" Trevor asked. "Or what your son did to Claudia? And me?"

"I'm sure you haven't forgotten any of that."

"Then what are you doing? You want to take me to a casino? For steak?"

"I suppose it's my way of apologizing. Trying to set things right. I'm a lawyer; I like the scales to balance."

What a terrifying person, Trevor thought, looking at Ridley. Could anyone in this man's life, anyone on this earth, divine whether he was telling the truth?

They crossed into Manhattan and when Trevor saw the tip of the Empire State Building he told Ridley he would pay back the $2,000 bail.

"Forget it, please," said Ridley.

"No offense," said Trevor, "but I don't want to be in debt to you."

"Stop. You act like I did something so horrible. I'm protecting my son. I'm sure your father would do the same."

Trevor decided to stop talking. He'd be home soon.

"I get how much you like Claudia," said Ridley when they pulled up to the curb outside the dorm. "But I want you to ask yourself this question: Is she really worth it? If she cared about you even half as much as you care about her she would have *at least* paid your bail. Has she called you since they found her? Texted?" Ridley saw the answer was no. "No. She's moved on. She used you, son. And now she's done with you. If it were me, I'd be pissed." He pulled out his business card. "I hear the NYPD wants to talk to you about Jeremy. I can help with that. As I'm sure you know, a good lawyer doesn't come cheap. What I'm hoping you'll do is keep me informed about Claudia. If you hear she or her family are thinking about going to the cops or the media, call me. I'll pay you $10,000 for a tip. Nobody wants that video out there, son. None of us."

"Fuck you, Ridley," said Trevor. He opened the door and climbed out of the low car and onto the sidewalk. "There is no 'us.'"

TREVOR

He returned to freshman life. What else could he do? When men with visitors' passes carried boxes out of Claudia's suite, Trevor said nothing. When someone in his Great American Cities class brought up what happened in the Mews and the conversation became about opioid abuse and gentrification, he said nothing. When Whitney gossiped about Claudia having a nervous breakdown, he said nothing. Whitney was easy to ignore if he didn't go to church. And he was done with church for a while.

"If you need Jesus we'll have Bible study here," said Boyd the Sunday night after Trevor's misadventure. They'd eaten stale pot gummies and were drinking what was left in the bladder of a box of wine Boyd brought home from a party.

"We'll do it all," continued Boyd, standing up, turning the conversation into a performance. Ad-libbing a monologue.

"Old Testament, New Testament. Eye for an eye, radical love. Everything."

"Great," said Trevor. "How about forgiveness? Can we do forgiveness?"

Boyd was the only person at school that Trevor told about Martha's Vineyard, and his roommate swore to keep the foolish pilgrimage to himself.

"Can we do forgiveness?" Boyd guffawed. "Christ *is* forgiveness."

It was good to laugh. For a moment he forgot about his heart, which felt a hundred years old. Life was now split into before and after spring break. Who he'd let himself become after seeing that video. What he'd done. What that meant. It was never going to go away.

"Praise Jesus," said Trevor, lifting the plastic cup for more.

When he woke up, hungover and hurting in the middle of the next afternoon, he had a text from Claudia.

hi. i hope you're okay. i know you probably wish you'd never met me, but I'm going to leave for the city for a while and i'd love to talk if you're willing.

Two hours later he was on East Twenty-Second Street. The town house Claudia lived in was almost as tall as Ben's brownstone, but where Ben's seemed to be hiding behind walls of ivy and spindly potted plants, hers stood out proudly, whitewashed brick and black shutters and a neat box of red geraniums outside each window.

The smile she greeted him with was mirthless, but sincere.

"It's good to see you," she said.

Claudia's hair was slightly damp, as if she'd just washed it. She shuffled inside in slippers and sweatpants. *You know a girl likes you if she dresses up a little*, Mike had told Trevor once. This was not going to be the beginning of their love story. What he'd done for her was humiliating. She was probably embarrassed by it, too.

They walked inside, into an enormous living room warmed by the sunlight coming from a wall of windows in the back. Just like at the house on Martha's Vineyard, the furniture and the lighting and the art and the knickknacks created a tableau: A successful family lives here. A healthy, happy family. But Trevor knew too much about the Castros now to be fooled.

"Do you want to go out to the garden?" she asked.

"Sure."

The garden was brick-paved, with a canopy of flowering trees above. A spiral staircase connected the patio to a balcony two floors above.

"This is nice," he said.

"Thanks."

She sat down in a cushioned outdoor armchair and he sat opposite her, at one end of the matching sofa.

"Are you coming back to school?" he asked.

"No, I'm gonna go to the Vineyard for a while."

"What about the fall?"

Claudia shook her head.

He didn't blame her. If he had her money he'd drop out, too.

"Have you told anybody?" she asked.

"I told my brother," he said

"I didn't know you had a brother." All they'd done together, and she didn't know basic details about his life. She hadn't asked and he hadn't offered. "What's his name?"

"He's not going to say anything."

"That's not what I meant," said Claudia.

"Well, he's not." Trevor was angrier than he wanted to be. She was never going to look at him the way he wanted her to. He was always going to be the person who'd been with her at the rock bottom of her life.

"I believe you." She looked down. "This is probably weird but I want to give you some money. To try and make it even. I mean, I know it'll never be even. Nothing's ever even. But if you'd given my phone to Ridley you'd have twenty thousand dollars. So I owe you twenty thousand dollars. That's how I see it."

Trevor wasn't surprised.

"Why didn't you just pay my bail?" he asked.

"What do you mean?"

"My bail. In Martha's Vineyard." Claudia looked confused. Was she playing dumb? "They arrested me for being at your house. They weren't going to let me out if I didn't pay two thousand dollars. That probably sounds like nothing to you but I don't have it. I don't think my parents do, either."

"I didn't know," she said quietly.

"You didn't know because you didn't care."

"That's not true. I told them I'd said you could be there. We told them to drop the charges."

"Okay, but did you, like, call to follow up? To make sure I wasn't still sitting in jail?"

"I didn't know I needed to."

He didn't say, *If it was Ben, you'd have made sure he was out. You'd have called and called until you knew he was free.* What did it matter now?

"I'm sorry," she said.

Trevor sighed. "It's okay." And maybe it was. Not good, not what he wanted, but okay. "I know you've got a lot to deal with."

"You could have called me," she said.

"I thought about it. But I didn't end up having to call anybody. Ridley Drake paid the bail. Then he drove me home." Claudia's mouth dropped open. "He's scared of you. He offered me ten thousand dollars for information about your family."

"What kind of information?"

"He wants to know if you're going to show the video to the cops or the media. I think he probably wants to be prepared. Get his lawyer-shit together. I told him to fuck off." He paused. "I don't think I should be taking money from any of you."

Claudia winced. "I get it."

City noises filled the silence that followed. An ambulance on a nearby street; the *rat-a-tat* of construction a few houses down.

"Have you heard anything about Jeremy?" Trevor asked.

"Sort of," she said, and told a story about Jeremy's brother at the Port Authority, and how he'd come to the town house, with a gun.

"Nobody got hurt," she said. "And the lawyer thinks it's actually kind of a good thing for us."

"Us?"

"You and me. Our security system has a picture of his brother on our stoop and his family knows that if they steer the cops our way, we'll report him for armed robbery. And our lawyer also says that the police don't have any footage of what happened in the Mews. So I think we're okay. I mean, I don't want you to worry. They don't have any proof of anything. If it comes to it, I'll say it was me. But it won't. Our lawyer used to be a DA. People owe her favors. So don't worry. Okay?"

Did she have any idea how she sounded? Was he supposed to trust her? Of course *she* didn't need to worry. Of course *she* was going to be fine. And maybe he would be, too. Maybe. But he had a feeling it would be a very long time before he stopped being afraid.

"Did Ridley say anything about Chad?" Claudia asked.

"Not really," said Trevor. "I saw his Instagram, though. I guess he's in L.A."

"I haven't been online."

"He's declared himself a victim of the Subway Slasher."

"What?"

Trevor took his phone out of his pocket and handed it to her. She scrolled and the color drained from her face.

"Sorry, I shouldn't have brought him up. I should probably go."

Claudia handed him his phone.

"Thanks for coming," she said. Thanks for everything. For being my friend. I don't know what I would have done without you."

"You might have called your family," he said. "Maybe that's what you should have done."

She smiled at him, another smile without joy. A smile beneath now-falling tears.

"Maybe."

CLAUDIA

As soon as she closed the door behind Trevor, Claudia went to her room and dug her phone from her bag. Since buying it in Midtown, she'd used it for almost nothing. She hadn't synched her email or her photos or her contacts. Trevor's new number was the only one programed. But now it was time to reenter the world.

She downloaded Instagram and sat on the edge of the bed, her blood hot and sputtering inside her like oil in a pan. Chad had posted four times since she'd left him bleeding in the hotel room ten days ago. The first was a photo of an IV stand in a hospital room. The caption read: *#nyc can suck my dick #recovery #subwayslasher #staystrong*. There were nearly six hundred likes and almost a hundred comments. *omg! . . . so crazy! . . . thoughts and prayers! . . . luv u!* The next photo was a vase of flowers with a "Get Well Soon" balloon attached; caption: *#blessed.* The third was a series of three female nurses posing like Charlie's Angels: *these bitches give good stitches.* And finally, the most recent: Chad's bare feet on a lounge chair with the ocean at his toes. *#Cali #bestcoast #recovery #staystrong.* Each post had more likes, more well-wishes.

She'd sliced him, in part, to create a warning. As she stood over him with the box cutter, she imagined that every time Chad Drake met someone new they'd be suspicious; what had he done to get such a dramatic injury? She'd thought she was changing the story, but she hadn't counted on how easy it would be for him to do the same. All those people on Instagram believed his lie about the Slasher. They felt sorry for him. He wasn't humiliated; he was a hero. Nobody would ask what he did to deserve it. Nobody would ask what he was wearing, or what he'd had to drink. *Poor Chad Drake was just in the wrong place at the wrong time.*

If she posted the video he made how many likes would she get? How many comments? Would she be a hero for surviving? No, she'd be a joke. *Dude, she peed.* It would be carved into her gravestone. What did she expect? She knew he liked her. She shouldn't have flirted. She shouldn't have had so much to drink. She should have known better.

Fine. Now she did. But she also knew she wouldn't be the last. She knew that if she didn't do something else—something, unfathomably, more than slicing him across the face—all she would have taught him was to be a little more careful when he wanted to fuck someone who didn't want to fuck him. Drop the camera, fly solo. How many women would he offer to drive home after they'd had three too many? *What a nice guy*, they'd think as he folded them into his fancy car. Out in L.A. his pool of victims would grow. What a story! He'd survived the Subway Slasher.

Claudia had to shut the door on all that. It wasn't enough to mark him in the dark. She couldn't leave anything open to interpretation. Symbolism was for critics and collectors; in real life, you have to point and say "rapist."

But say it to who? The police? Ridley would get any charges dropped to nothing: Chad would end up picking up trash on Park Avenue every other weekend. Ten years from now, people who knew him would refer to the whole thing as a bit of youthful legal trouble. A reformed bad boy and boom: a whole new set of women ready to comfort him. A whole new set of victims.

Claudia put the phone face down on the bed. In a frame across the room was a charcoal drawing of a dancer she'd done the year before in high school. Most of her art classes had focused on "fine art," art for art's sake, but spring semester of senior year the studio teacher decided everyone needed something "practical" in their portfolios to graduate. Each student was assigned a client—a club or group or team at school—and told to create an image, one version on paper, one digital, that functioned as an advertisement for their performance or product or big game. Claudia was paired with the dance troupe who wanted to spread the word about their graduation show, proceeds to support Ballet Bushwick. She attended rehearsal after rehearsal, trying to get inspired, trying to come up with something to *say* about what their movements meant or at least what they evoked. She went to the Bushwick studio and took photographs, collected bits of ribbon and chalk; a Band-Aid, even a condom wrapper she saw in the bathroom trash can. She took it all home and came up with nothing. In the end, she turned in a simple charcoal drawing of a dancer, arms raised; the only flourish was her gold dance slippers—glitter nail polish on the original that she presented in class. She'd basically drawn a Degas and sprinkled Damien Hirst at its feet.

The teacher praised her.

"This is smartly done," she'd said. "You're most skilled at sketch and I like that you stuck with that. Commercial work isn't about taking big chances or showing off. It isn't about you at all, other than that they've hired you and, presumably, like your aesthetic. It's about the client. How do you best use your skills to please the client? Have the dancers seen this?"

Claudia answered yes.

"And?"

"They like it," she said.

"But you don't."

Claudia shrugged. She wanted to make Art. She could identify it, she was drawn to it, and she could pay for it—but she couldn't seem to create it. She excelled at figure drawing and still life. If it was there in front of her she could imitate its contours. What she couldn't do was bring it to life. The dancer on her wall conveyed a sense of movement, maybe even grace, but she couldn't manage to blow a spirit into what she drew. Nothing she'd ever made—not her tries at sculpture and mixed media, watercolor, or photography—

opened anyone's eyes any wider. Real artists could show you the truth you hadn't noticed. Real artists had something to say.

Well, thought Claudia as she picked up her phone and looked once more at Chad's Instagram, I may never be a real artist, but I definitely have something to say.

She walked to her desk and awoke the sleeping computer with a wag of the mouse. In the bag she'd taken to Poughkeepsie was her old cell phone, the one Chad sent the video to. She connected the phone to the computer and uploaded the video. The opening image was the close-up of her mouth. When she'd first seen it, the sensation that shot through her cells was rooted in shame. *What did I do*? She remembered squeezing her eyes shut, banging and banging on that black door in her mind. *Did I agree to that?* But watching it now, it was so clear: She might as well have been a dead body. Her slack and sloppy face was embarrassing; it was going to haunt her forever. But what stood out to her this time was not her expression, it was Chad's. His smile was one of triumph. The smile of a man who couldn't contain his glee. A man utterly unburdened by the experience of anyone else in the room, in the world.

She froze the video on that smile and cropped herself out. The image now was just Chad, naked from the waist up, his grinning face in the foreground, the dorm room blurry behind him. She connected her Bluetooth pen and drew the word across his chest in red. Too obvious? Now her mind was going. There was an artist in Brooklyn who drew the same outline of herself as a stick figure on walls and windows and discarded furniture all over the city. Beneath each she'd write a short phrase; usually something that referenced the object she was drawing on. *Let me comfort you* on a mattress; *I need time for reflection* on a mirror. Claudia's professor had assigned an article about her as part of a discussion of the "meme-ification" of street art. The class was of varying opinions on whether the messages were sufficiently thoughtful to be considered "art" but the one thing you couldn't question was her reach: Millions of people had seen her work. Reach was what Claudia wanted now. Chad Drake was about to become a meme.

She saved the image as ChadRape.jpeg, then erased the word and started over, this time drawing a dialogue bubble beside his face:

Hey bro! Is it rape if she can't walk?

She saved it as Bro1.jpeg, then clicked back to the original and did it again.

Hey bro! Is it rape if she can't talk?

Hey bro! Is it rape if she can't remember?

Hey bro! Is it rape if she's a slut?

Hey bro! Is it rape if I don't get caught?

In ten minutes she had seven images; one with words in an old-fashioned typewriter font; one with letters that mimicked the newspaper cut-outs of a ransom note; one scrawled in digital lipstick. She printed out a copy of each and set up a new Instagram account: BroChadAsks. She uploaded the first image with the hashtag #isitrape. For now, BroChad asked about rape. But who knew? Maybe that would change.

She sent copies of each image to her email; there was a twenty-four-hour copy center off Union Square. She could have them printed there—large-format, on canvas or vinyl; the perfect size for posting on subway walls and building sides. She'd make a thousand 8.5 × 11 copies. She would stand in the middle of Times Square and throw them into the air. She would hand them out to people eating dinner at outdoor cafes, go to the dorm and put one in every student mailbox. Chad Drake would be tagged and vandalized; people would spill on him, piss on him, vomit on him. Laugh at him.

Claudia put on jeans and a black sweater and laced up her high-tops. She brushed her teeth and brushed her hair and saw in the mirror that the last trace of the eye injury was gone. *No one would ever know*, she thought. And that, of course, was the problem.

She knocked on Edie's door before she left.

"Come in," said her sister.

The room was dark—Edie had been sleeping. "I'm sorry," said Claudia.

"No, it's cool." Edie sat up and smiled. The family had let Claudia ghost around since they brought her back from Poughkeepsie. Nobody asked her to do anything except meet with the lawyer. Her mom suggested therapy but didn't insist. It was probably a good idea "Are you going somewhere?"

"Where's Lydia?"

"Nathan's got her. We're doing six-hour shifts."

"How are you?"

Edie rolled her eyes, yawned. "I'm just glad you're okay."

"I'm sorry you guys were so worried."

"I wish you'd told me. I would have done anything you needed."

"I needed you to give me a break," said Claudia. "I needed the benefit of the doubt."

Edie nodded, her eyes teared up. "Right."

Claudia sat down and put her hand on her sister's leg. She was not going to apologize, at least not now. But she also wasn't going to stay mad. Edie hadn't done anything wrong, either.

"I forgive you if you forgive me," Claudia said.

"There's nothing to forgive."

"I missed Lydia."

"You didn't miss her," said Edie. "She's here, you're here."

Claudia pulled out her phone and showed Edie the Instagram. BroChadAsks had 18 followers, 63 likes, and one comment: *Yes!*

"I wish you could come with me," said Claudia after she told Edie what she was planning. "But I think it might be illegal and you probably shouldn't get arrested now that you're a mom."

"I'll walk you to Union Square," said Edie.

"Yeah?"

"Yeah. It's just a walk, right?"

"Right," said Claudia. But it wasn't just a walk and they both knew it. It was love.

Claudia waited for her sister on the front stoop. From behind Trevor's sunglasses she watched the people hurrying along the block with their dogs and their strollers and their shopping bags; talking into unseen earpieces, locked into their phones. Had any of them seen her post yet?

Edie came outside, wrapping an oversized sweater around her stomach. Her belly was still round and Claudia imagined that her sister was a little self-conscious. She thought about what Trevor had said; what if she'd just called her family instead of latching on to him?

"Did you tell them?" Claudia asked.

"Mom and Dad? No. Of course I didn't."

"Is this stupid?"

"I don't think so. I mean, it's art, right? What's Ridley going to do—sue you? That'll just make more people pay attention."

"I could make a series of him, too," Claudia said. "What he did to you is almost as bad."

"No it's not," said Edie. "But thanks."

They stopped at a crosswalk as a fire truck screamed by. Claudia had held her ears against that sound since childhood, but she let it smash into her eardrums today. It was a different pain than the one in her heart and for a moment it made her forget.

"Does this mean you're going to go to the police?" asked Edie as they approached the copy store.

"Maybe," said Claudia. She'd looked it up online: In New York State victims had twenty-five years to report their rapists. "Or maybe after all this, they'll come to me."

ACKNOWLEDGMENTS

I've said it before and I'll say it again: the most profound privilege of being a published author is the opportunity to work with talented people who care about your writing. In my case, I have a dream team. Thank you, first and foremost, to my agent, Stephanie Kip Rostan. I don't think this book would exist without your constant support and guidance, your honest advice, and your bold ideas. Thank you to Courtney Paganelli of Levine Greenberg Rostan for being one of the best brainstorming companions I've ever had. And thank you to Kelley Ragland at Minotaur for your patience, your trust, and your brilliant notes.

Thank you to Laura Lippman for providing time and space to write. And thank you to my writing buddies, Katherine Dykstra, Laura McHugh, and Adam Sternbergh, for the countless conversations, emails, texts, and DMs that kept my spirits up and my focus on the final product—no matter how far away it sometimes seemed.

Thank you to my readers: Katie Brown, Barbara Dahl, Erin Donaghue, Laura McHugh, and Susan Dahl Sharer. Thank you to Danielle Citron, Allison Leotta, Andrea Pino-Silva, and Amy Telsey for your expertise.

Thank you to my girlfriends: Melissa Tepe, Liora Brener Fogelman, Emmy Betz, Heidi Altman, and Naomi Walcott. Your friendship has sustained me for more than two decades and your encouragement as I struggled with this book buoyed me when I needed it most.

Thank you to my parents, Barbara and Bill Dahl, for giving me the rare and precious gift of a happy childhood.

Thank you to my husband, Joel Bukiewicz: marrying you was the best decision I've ever made. Thank you to my sister-in-law, Lori Bukiewicz, for taking such good care of my son (and me) while I wrote. And thank you to my son, Mick Bukiewicz, for expanding my heart and blowing my mind every single day.

This book is dedicated to my sister, Susan Dahl Sharer, who has had my back for forty-two years. You've always known the meaning of sisterhood, puss, even when I couldn't quite figure it out.